CW01207719

Blinded No More

NANCY A. WISEMAN

Blinded No More
Copyright © 2023 by Nancy A. Wiseman

All rights reserved. No part of this publication may be reproduced, distributed, or transmitted in any form or by any means, including photocopying, recording, or other electronic or mechanical methods, without the prior written permission of the author, except in the case of brief quotations embodied in critical reviews and certain other non-commercial uses permitted by copyright law.

tellwell

Tellwell Talent
www.tellwell.ca

ISBN
978-1-77941-277-5 (Hardcover)
978-1-77941-276-8 (Paperback)
978-1-77941-278-2 (eBook)

Dedication

This novel is dedicated to my children, Caleigh and John Will, who I know without question are the two best decisions I have ever made and are the two greatest joys of my life. You both inspire me.

To my best friend, Lisa, you have been the supportive rock by my side since we were teenagers. You are the kind of friend everyone deserves to have, and I am so thankful we chose each other. You encourage and lift me through all my decisions. Thank you for all your valuable insight after reading my first draft.

To the champion of my writing dream, I am thankful for you, Kara. You gave me a journal to write down my novel notes and had your mom knit me a blanket for something comforting and warm while I wrote. Having you there at my first reading of personal work gave me the confidence that I had something worthwhile to share.

To my Mom in heaven, you instilled the strength in me to never give up, to go after my dreams, and no matter what happens in life, to always find the positive and keep moving forward.

Acknowledgement from Editor Jules Hucke

Nancy, you've made absolutely phenomenal changes since the first draft; your hard work to improve your craft is evident on every page! I'm so impressed by how much you've grown as a writer in such a short time. Amazing!

CHAPTER 1

The Catalyst

                                                      ∽

THE RING OF her cell phone in the middle of the night jolted Cara from a deep sleep. Slapping at the edge of her nightstand trying to find it in the dark, her fingertips hit the rubber cover. Clasping it, she brought it to her ear. "Hello."

"This is Father Patrick's Care Centre. It's time. You need to be here now."

The night nurse's voice was not recognizable to Cara's foggy brain, but the words were. Springing out of bed, sweat coating her body, Cara fumbled in the darkness for the light switch. The brightness blinded her as she threw on a pair of jeans and a sweater before bolting down the hall to the stairs.

Please, God, don't let her die alone.

Racing up the stairs to the main floor, she was thankful that Dani and Cody were at sleepovers. Passing her husband Jay's bedroom, the silence was deafening with his all-too-familiar absence. He was probably on his sixth pint of Keith's, out with friends she had never met. How long had it been since they had done anything as a couple—two, maybe two and a half years now? She knew she was no longer his shining light.

Outside, the October night's unexpected warmth felt suffocating, like the looming thoughts of where she was headed. Shifting the car into gear and heading up the long asphalt driveway, Cara glanced into the rear-view mirror to see the large leafless poplar trees swallowed into the darkness.

Cara could have done this twenty-minute drive blindfolded. Speeding through every light, whether green, yellow, or red, she was okay with breaking the rules this one time. She had to make it to the Care Centre before it was too late.

She'd known the call was coming, but that didn't make it any easier. *Whatever you do, Cara, don't be late.* When had she ever been late?

Vibrating at the glass front entrance waiting for the buzz to allow her in, Cara was sure her thunderous heartbeats would shatter the glass if the door didn't unlock soon. Bursting into the familiar antiseptic smell of the pale green hallways, hearing only the sound of her rubber soles squeaking against the freshly polished floors, Cara took one deep breath, exhaling. *You can do this, Cara,* she told herself before entering her dying mom's room.

Cara winced at the reality of what Alzheimer's had taken away. Gone was the beautiful, vibrant soul with a positive attitude and outlook. Gone was the strong, independent woman who always made the best of every situation, wearing a smile even in difficult times. In place lay a pale, pronounced, skeletal frame, cheeks hollowed, only her chest showing that a molecule of her mom was still there as her ribs slowly rose and fell below the soft pink nighty, with each laboured breath.

Shaking her head from side to side, "Why, Mom? Why like this?"

Inhale…exhale.

Tenderly kissing her forehead, Cara shivered. "I got you, Mom." She pulled the thick white quilted comforter up from the bottom of the bed, exposing bright, colourful printed flowers as it unfolded. Dragging the paisley-patterned La-Z-Boy chair as close as possible to her mom's bedside, Cara sat, placing her mom's hand in hers and stroking it ever so gently. "You're not alone, Mom. I made it. I'm here."

Inhale…exhale.

"I can't believe six years have come and gone since Dad passed and I brought you halfway across Canada to Calgary to live with us. I tried my best, Mom, to make the transition for you as easy as possible by setting up your new bedroom to look just like your old one, with soft yellow walls, your furniture, knickknacks, and family photos. I wanted things to feel familiar and comforting for you. I knew I'd done the right thing when you shared with me that the heaviness in your stomach was gone, and you felt safe in your new home."

Inhale…exhale.

"Mom, I'm so glad you were able to spend so many special moments with my family. Having you be part of the birthday parties, the kids' school concerts, and sporting events was such a blessing for us all. I loved watching how excited you got at Dani's basketball games, cheering so loud when she would complete a free throw. It was so cute seeing you jump up and holler, "Way to go, Cara," thinking it was me because I too wore number three when you watched me play ball as a kid. Last Christmas was a little tough when you no longer understood that the present sitting on your lap was something special for you, but that was okay, Mom. You were with us, and that's all that mattered."

Inhale…exhale.

Cara reached out her hand to softly touch her Mom's cheek. She remembered as a child how her Mom would do the same thing to her before kissing her goodnight.

"Wasn't it fun, Mom when we went on all our road trips together? It always made me giggle, to catch you randomly humming as we drove down the highway. I wondered what was going through your mind. Were you thinking about all the trips across Canada you took with Dad, or were you just happy to be out and about? I know you enjoyed visiting all those little towns we went to, especially walking through the musty antique stores in Nanton. Without fail, you'd say to me every time, 'This place smells just like Grandma's.' Oh, Mom, how I wish I could hear you say those words one more time." Cara closed her eyes and gingerly squeezed her Mom's hand.

"You sure did love Bill's Drive Inn, for your favourite maple walnut ice cream. One big scoop balanced inside a waffle cone. I miss how your eyes always looked at me so lovingly when I would wipe the dripping ice cream from your chin."

Inhale...exhale.

"We've shared so much life together, Mom, and I want you to know how much I love you and how lucky I feel that you were my mom. I've never shared this with you, but the greatest gift you ever gave me was knowing I could always count on you."

A momentary smile broke out on Cara's face as she recalled a memory from university. "Like when I was dating Jay, Mom, and had planned to stay overnight with him for the first time. This story, I've shared so many times with friends because it was just so sweet how you took it upon yourself to sneak out late that night to make fresh footprints in the snow, so when Dad headed to work, it would look like I had left early that morning for school. You were always there for me, Mom. If I needed you, you showed up. If I was worried about anything, you talked me through it. If I needed someone to listen, you made yourself available. You made me feel that I was important to you. You made me feel safe and loved. You always had my back, especially with you-know-who."

Inhale...exhale.

Cara had watched for years as the unforgiving claws of Alzheimer's slowly embedded into her mom's brain. Day after day, it stole memory after memory until just a shell of her mom was left.

"I'm forty-four, Mom, and I'm so scared of ending up alone."

Inhale…

"Oh God, no, not yet!" Cara clasped her mom's hand tightly to her chest. "I'm not ready, Mom!"

Vice grips tightened on Cara's heart to the beat of each stuttered breath she gulped, as she fought to control her emotions. She found a smidgeon of peace knowing her mom was no longer in the debilitating hold of Alzheimer's, but it wasn't enough to outweigh what had been taken away from her for the second and final time.

It was the sound of the train whistle outside that caused Cara to open her eyes and release the strangling grip she had on her mom's hand. Beyond the window, a predawn grey was turning to a clear blue, brightening the room. From as early on as Cara could remember, she had always loved the sound of a train. The whistle blew once again, letting her know it was drawing near. The screech of the metal wheels against the metal rails grew louder and louder the closer it got. That sound always gave Cara a comforting feeling, a feeling of home.

Tap, tap, tap…

Cara rose from her chair and walked toward the widow as a shimmering blue dragonfly bounced outside the windowpane. Its translucent wings, outlined in black, fluttered in the rising sun's rays. Mesmerized and feeling a sense of oneness, Cara placed her hand against the glass only to watch as the dragonfly flew away, disappearing into the new day.

"Goodbye, Mom."

CHAPTER 2

Lila

"It feels surreal being back home, Lila. Thank you for being here with me."

"What are best friends for? I can't believe none of your brothers flew back. Damien still lives in town, doesn't he?"

"He does, but he doesn't even know I'm back."

"What? You're spreading your parents' ashes. Shouldn't he be here?"

The thought of having Damien anywhere near her made her skin crawl. It would have been nice if her other brothers could have made the trip, but nope, just like when their youngest brother, died from heart failure at only thirty-one, not one of her three brothers living in the same city as him took care of the arrangements. Cara was the one who jumped on a plane, coordinated the funeral, set up the cremation, and took care of all the paperwork.

"I picked out a song, Lila, called 'Dancing in the Sky,' to play while I spread my mom's and dad's ashes. Since they both loved to dance with one another, I thought it fitting for today. Would you mind holding my phone while it plays?"

"You bet I will! I know this song. It's perfect, Cara."

Cara's cheeks were the only part of her exposed to the crisp November morning. She was thankful for her forethought to have thrown a scarf into her luggage at the last minute. Even though the frost was building on the scarf from the plumes of her breath, and it was a bit scratchy under her chin, the feeling it provided of an extra hug on such a dreary day outweighed any discomfort. Leaves crackled under frozen dew as she and Lila walked among the hundreds of trees her parents had painstakingly planted over the years on the small piece of land they owned, only thirty minutes from their family home in Thunder Bay, Ontario.

"When was the last time you were here?"

"I'd have to think about that, Lila. The trees were only up to my waist then."

"Those trees are like thirty feet now!"

"I used to run through them when I was little with my five older brothers playing tag and hide-and-seek. We would roast marshmallows over that old firepit, and see the hill. That's where we would toboggan. It seemed so much steeper back then." Some childhood memories had been great…Cara shook her head briskly to rid herself of the ones that weren't.

"Why did you choose to do it here?"

"My parents used to call this place their little piece of heaven. Their final wish for when both of them had passed, was to have their ashes mixed and spread on their land. I promised I would do it, and here we are. So glad you're here with me, Lila. Thank you for always being such an amazing friend."

"Of course, you'd do the same for me."

"You know I would." Cara's brow furrowed as she fumbled with the lid, trying to unscrew it. "Damn it; my fingers are so cold."

"Can I help?"

"Thank you, Lila, but I'll get it." After a few more attempts, the lid finally gave way. Wanting to delay the inevitable, Cara took a few extra moments to ponder her next move. She ran her index finger around the metal rim a few times, goosebumps instantly rising beneath her clothes. It was now or never. Cara forced her hand into the canister, grabbing the first handful. Flour came to mind, cool to the touch, only grittier, heavier. The funeral director's unemotional voice was next to pop into her thoughts: *Careful not to breathe in the ashes. There are bone fragments, and they won't dissolve well if you do.* "What is it people say, Lila, ashes to ashes, dust to dust? Or is it, for dust you are, and to dust you will return?"

"I think anything you say will be perfectly fine."

Her parents' Adirondack chairs seemed the right place to start, as Cara remembered her parents in those chairs drinking coffee freshly made over the campfire her dad had lit every time with only one match. With her hand no longer protected from the elements, Cara spread her fingers, letting her mom and dad glide across and settle on the faded flecks of old red paint and wet wood. The ash-coated chairs now looked more like side-by-side tombstones in an overgrown gravesite. Moving among the pine trees, spreading some of their ashes here and there, Cara slowly made her way toward the weather-rusted school bus. The story her mom had told her was that her dad had bought it secondhand through his teaching connections with the Catholic school board and then modified it by removing almost all the bench seats so their family of eight would have a place to sleep during their weekend campouts. It sat much lower to the ground now, tires flat, a quarter of the rims embedded in the soil from all the years it had sat there. Hearing the music helped push her forward with the repetitive motion of flinging out the ashes. With a final slap to the bottom of the urn, the last of her parents' remains dislodged, the wind finishing the job. Tilting her head upward, Cara softly whispered, "Goodbye Mom and Dad I hope the two of you are dancing together in heaven."

Lila wrapped her arm around Cara's shoulders. "How are you holding up, my friend?"

"I'm okay, just ready to go now."

As they made their way back to the car, Cara's nose crinkled at the musky, sweet smell emanating from the rotting leaves mushing together under her feet.

"Every time I'm back on this stretch of road, Lila, I forget how beautiful the drive is."

"It is, isn't it? The sun shining down on the Kaministiquia River is beautiful at this time of day. Lila turned her head back toward Cara, "How long has it been now since we've known each other, Cara?"

"Gee, I think like twenty-seven, maybe twenty-eight years?"

"We're getting old!"

"It seems like yesterday when we met working in the video department at Sears."

"You were still in high school."

"I was enamoured with you back then, Lila."

"Enamoured with me? Why?"

"You were three years older; you owned a car, smoked cigarettes, and went dancing at the Landmark on weekends. When I hung out with you, I got to colour outside the lines."

"We sure did have some fun back then, didn't we? I'm not that same gal anymore, Cara. The wildness has quieted, and I'm in bed by nine now." Breaking out her beautiful warm smile.

Cara giggled. "Your bedtime might have changed, but you're still the same loving Lila I've always known."

"You're too kind, Cara. Hey, I've been holding off telling you something because I wanted to wait until you got through everything with your folks. I think now's the time to share my great news with you and I'm pretty sure it's going to brighten your spirits."

"Don't keep me waiting."

"You aren't going to believe it, but I'm getting transferred to Calgary."

"Oh my God, Lila, you just made my year!"

"When the head-hunter came a-knocking, the offer was just too good to pass up." She winked at Cara. "It also didn't hurt that my closest friend lives there."

"This is truly the best news, and trust me, it couldn't have come at a better time."

"There's nothing here for me anymore now that Robert's gone."

"His funeral was the last time I was back home, Lila. That was almost three years ago. Does it get easier with time?

"Time helps, but I don't think I'll ever get over losing him. His heart attack blind-sided me. I always thought he would go before me because of our ten-year age difference, but I never thought I would lose him as early as I did. He was my everything, my ride or die."

Cara reached over and placed her hand on Lila's squeezing it. "You and Robert were like me and my mom. We both had a very special bond."

Lila sat back and held her hand to her chest. Her breaths became quick as she struggled to get air into her lungs.

"Are you okay? I'm so sorry for talking about Robert."

Lila knew it wasn't thoughts of Robert that had her chest feeling like it was about to explode.

"Do you need me to pull over?"

"I'll be okay." Not believing her own words. "I just need a few moments to catch my breath."

As they entered the city limits, Cara was the first to speak. "Are you feeling any better? You frightened me."

"I frightened myself. That's never happened to me before but I feel okay now."

"Thank goodness," reaching over and rubbing Lila's shoulder.

Wanting the subject to change, Lila asked. "You're flying home tomorrow, right?"

"Yes, a late afternoon flight and now that I know you're moving, there's no reason for me to ever come back, so there's one last thing I want to do in the morning before I leave."

"Do you need my help?"

"Thanks for the offer, Lila, but this is something I need to take care of on my own."

CHAPTER 3

Him

~~~

THE PARKING LOT at the only mall in Thunder Bay was quite full for a Sunday morning. Cara had chosen to meet here instead of the food court, where he thought they should meet… like she was going to do what he wanted. Never again! Today, the temperature was below freezing for the second day in a row, and no matter how high she blasted the heat in her parents' sky-blue Chevrolet truck, she couldn't shake the chill or the shivers.

Milling over what she was going to say caused the choked-down memories to come pounding back like a jackhammer breaking away at cement. The box she had so carefully constructed in her mind all those years ago to stuff the horror into was cracking open.

There he was. Cara fidgeted in her seat as she watched him walk toward the truck. He looked different. His shoulders were no longer broad, instead hunched now with his hands deep in his coat pockets, not once making eye contact with her. He was close enough now to see the thick cop moustache peppered with grey. The buttons on his jacket were stretched to the max as if a basketball was hidden underneath the fabric. His presence wasn't intimidating anymore; he just looked old.

Cara sat taller in her seat. He slid in, eyes never leaving the dashboard. As soon as he'd closed the door Cara spoke. "I wanted to meet this morning because I need to talk about what you did to me as a child."

Under his breath, Damien said, "Something happened to me with a priest." He was prepared like he knew this day had finally arrived.

"Whatever happened, you had a choice with me. You were my big brother. You were supposed to protect me!"

Cara noticed the tremble in his hands, but he wasn't saying anything. He was sitting there looking at his damn feet like they had all the answers.

"Our Catholic background makes me feel I should forgive you, but I want you to know that you will never be welcome in my home, and you will never meet my kids."

Nothing. He still wasn't saying anything! He wasn't even apologizing!

Cara slammed her hands on the steering wheel. "God damn you, Damien, I was only seven. You were twenty-two."

"Does anyone know?"

Cara's veins throbbed in her temples as she shouted, "Mom knew, you bastard! That's why it stopped when I was ten. I couldn't even say the words out loud to her because I was so embarrassed and ashamed. I wrote it all in a note and gave it to her. I told her everything you had been doing to me. I told her all the secrets you told me to keep."

Silence.

"I'd never seen Mom cry, but I did that day. Through her tears she just kept repeating, 'I'm so sorry baby, I'm so sorry. I'll never leave you alone with him again.' She's the only one I told. She didn't want anyone else to know because she was afraid if Dad found out, he would kill you."

Nothing. Still nothing.

"Was I the only one? Did you ever touch your daughter?"

"I would never have touched her; I love her."

Those three words cut like a knife plunged deep into the center of her gut, slowly and methodically slicing from the left side to the right, leaving no room for error in what he had meant.

"You need to leave, Damien. Get out of this truck. I never want to see you again."

CHAPTER 4

Jay

THE GRASS, ONCE richly green, now looked beige out the window. Cara sat in a haze behind the mahogany desk of her home office. She'd been back for over a week now, and no matter how hard she tried, she couldn't shake the sadness that enveloped her like a thick fog.

"God, I miss you, Mom."

Her business paperwork usually sat in neat, organized piles, prioritized and ready to be tackled, but now it was strewn across her desk. She couldn't concentrate and knew her real estate investment work would have to wait as she had a much more pressing issue that needed to be addressed now, so she could start moving forward, back to her happy self. She knew it would be difficult, but nothing would get better if she didn't change how she had lived these last two years. The magnet that had drawn her and Jay together over two decades ago had lost its charge. They were nothing more than roommates now, and not good roommates at that.

It was such a vast difference from when they'd first met in university all those years ago. Back then, they were tighter than superglue. Cara remembered their first meeting at the 'Study' pub on campus. She and Lila had found seats against the back wall that night, positioned perfectly to check out the entire bar scene. Students gathered in one corner, watching their friends play *Pac-Man* and *Centipede*. Close by, an intense game of pool was being played. The losing player pulled at his hair as he watched his opponent's last ball drop. Just outside the bathroom doors was a narrow wall where a dartboard hung. Cara had never understood how mixing alcohol and sharp pointy flying objects was smart and always wondered how people didn't walk out of bars with darts stuck in various parts of their bodies.

Lila waved down their server, who quickly returned with two tall glasses of ice-cold draught beer and a shaker of salt. Almost as soon as they clinked their glasses and swallowed their first sip, the lights dimmed, and the DJ started pumping out the tunes.

Halfway through her beer, Cara looked up to see a tall, shaggy-haired boy pointing to the empty barstool beside her, asking if the seat was taken. She was instantly drawn to his boyish good looks, striking hazel eyes, and charismatic smile, and welcomed him to take the seat. The immediate attraction surprised Cara. She had never experienced those feelings. Whenever she had gone out with guys in high school, which wasn't often, there was never a real connection and it always felt like she was going through the motions. She had even asked her mom why she didn't feel anything when she kissed different boys. Her mom assured her it would be completely different when the right one came along.

After only an hour of sitting and laughing with Jay, Cara finally understood what her mom had meant. The butterflies were there with Jay.

As the weeks and months passed, he was on her mind morning, noon, and night. When Cara graduated, they married, and both landed great jobs in Calgary. Jay an Architect and Cara, a marketing position with an oil and gas company. They loved to travel together, and on one of those holidays, eleven years into their marriage, Cara knew before walking across the street in Phuket, Thailand, to buy a pregnancy test from the drugstore, that her suspicion of being pregnant was indeed true. Dani arrived nine months later, followed by Cody twenty-three months after her. Cara loved Jay deeply, never thinking she would be without him, but time and circumstance changed all that. Today, she needed to pull up her big girl panties and do what needed to be done.

As she walked into Jay's vehicle and woodworking shop attached to their acreage home, sweat dripped down her back, even though the room was slightly cool. She found Jay sitting beside his '69 burgundy Corvette, polishing one of the rims. The lemony cleaning foam was a pleasant smell for the unpleasant moment she was about to embark on. "Do you have a minute to talk with me?"

Without even looking up, Jay grunted a muffled, "Sure."

They took seats across from each other at the bar table. *Just say it, Cara. There's no way to soften this blow.* "We need to talk about us, Jay."

He didn't reply. He folded his arms across his chest and leaned back against the wall.

Cara swallowed hard, trying to produce saliva so her tongue would unstick from the roof of her mouth. "We've been putting off the inevitable, and it's time we discuss our marriage issues." It took everything in Cara to continue because she saw the pain in Jay's eyes. *Take a deep breath, Cara, and rip the Band-Aid off.* "I haven't been happy for a long time, Jay, and I don't believe you have been either. Please know I am not saying any of this to be hurtful, but I know in my heart that I can't continue living the way we have been. It isn't healthy or fair to you, the kids, or me. We haven't been living like a married couple, yet we still celebrated our twentieth wedding anniversary, pretending in front of our children, family, and friends that we were still happy and in love."

Jay's eyes glazed with unshed tears.

"Posing together so your mom could take a picture of the day was my final straw. All I could think at that moment was, *What the heck am I doing?*" Cara had always been a truthful person, and to stand there all smiles with their arms around each other, making it look like all was great, was something she was no longer willing to do. "You and I both know our feelings have changed toward each other, and it's time we talk about how we truly feel so that things can get better for both of us." Deep breath in, "I've fallen out of love with you, Jay."

His shoulders dropped.

Cara continued, "Day after day, you go to work, and night after night, you're always out."

Silence.

"For a long time, it's felt like it's just the kids and me. It doesn't even feel like you are part of our lives anymore. Having my mom living with us and then your mom, after your dad passed last year, has taken a toll on us, and our marriage has suffered the brunt of it. We've been dealing with all these things in our own way instead of working through them together."

Jay placed his hands on the table only to readjust them to his lap, leaving foggy handprints fading on the table.

"I tried to involve you in our daily lives, Jay, and bring issues to your attention, but all I got from you was anger. You didn't support me; you just got mad and left. Having to take care of our two kids, deal with your mom and her mourning, and spend time at the care centre to be there for my mom has been extremely overwhelming and hard on me. Not having you around to bear some of the load has not been fair. You don't have my back anymore, Jay."

"I stayed away and worked crazy-long hours because it was what I needed to do, to get me through my days."

"You dealt with your stress the way you needed to, Jay, and I dealt with it by internalizing and then exploding on you when I couldn't keep it in any longer."

"You're right, Cara; we can't continue like this. Where will we all live? What about the kids? What about our business?"

"I'll start looking for a place for the kids and me. I want them full-time, Jay, because that's what's best for them. They can spend every second weekend with you, and if you want more time during the week, we'll make it work. We don't need to worry about spousal or child support because our rental property business brings in enough that we both can live comfortably."

"I never wanted this to happen to us, Cara, but it needs to happen. I don't want to waste money on lawyers or dissolve our company, so why don't we keep running things as we have, and we can share our assets for now until we figure things out."

"That sounds perfect, Jay. Thank you for hearing me."

Cara walked back to her bedroom suite with mixed emotions. Even though she knew ending her marriage was the right thing to do, she felt the heaviness of failure. Failure on her part for no longer wanting to put in the effort to make her marriage work. She had always thought Jay would be her person for life, but now that was no longer the case.

CHAPTER 5

Dani & Cody

CARA HAD ALWAYS had an open dialogue about anything with Dani and Cody, but this was different; this was a conversation no parent ever wanted to have with their kids. Just like everything regarding the family, the onus had been left on her. There were times over the past two weeks when she thought she would tell them, but her gut told her to wait as the time didn't feel right. Tonight, though, was perfect. Jay had a pickup hockey game with his buddies, so a movie night at home felt like the right place and time to tell them. When the kids settled in on Dani's bed with their bowls of popcorn drizzled in butter, Cara said, "There's something I've been wanting to discuss with both of you."

Ten-year-old Dani and eight-year-old Cody looked at her quizzically.

"I want the two of you to know that I love you both so much."

Cody elbowed Dani. "Mom loves me more!"

Dani returned the jab. "Ya, whatever you want to believe, Cody."

"Come on, kids, Mamma has something to share with you."

"Ya, Dani." Cody poked her.

"I know you have seen me sleeping downstairs for a while now instead of being upstairs with your dad. I've chosen to do that because my feelings have changed for him, and I'm no longer in love with your dad anymore."

Dani and Cody stopped squirming. Neither moved a muscle, and both kept constant eye contact with their mom.

"Your dad and I've talked, and I let him know that because I'm no longer in love with him, I can't be with him anymore. I need you both to know that my leaving him has nothing to do with either of you. Your dad and I love the two of you more than anything in this world, and no matter what we're going through, our love for both of you will never change."

Neither one of them moved or said a word.

"I don't want either one of you to blame your dad for us separating. This was my decision, and I take full responsibility for making this choice." Cara stopped and waited. She wanted to give Dani and Cody time to let what she was saying sink in.

Cody spoke. "Mom, I'm not happy that you are going to leave Dad, but I can understand you not wanting to be with someone you are not in love with anymore."

Cody's words dumbfounded Cara. How did her little boy get so wise? His comforting words made her tear up.

Dani sat quietly, but Cara could see her wheels turning by her concentrated expression.

Cara leaned in closer to hold their hands. "I want you kids to know that when you're married to someone, you always try to think of that person first. That person is the one you want to spend all your time with. You want to show affection to them by touching their hand, kissing them, and telling them you love them. They should be doing the same to you too." Cara knew she hadn't felt that way or shown any of those emotions toward Jay for a very long time and had been riddled with guilt thinking her kids might grow up thinking a loveless marriage was normal. "Do either one of you have any questions?"

Dani piped up. "I'm okay with your decision, Mamma, but are we going to have another dad?"

"That's one thing you two will not have to worry about. I don't have plans to ever be married again."

"When you and Dad don't live together anymore, where will we live?" Cody asked.

"You and Dani will be living full-time with me, but you'll stay with your dad every second weekend because he wants to spend time with you, too."

Dani and Cody grew quiet again.

"I know this is a lot for both of you to process right now, so if you want to talk later, I will answer any questions you may have. Make a little space for Mamma so I can sit between the two of you for the movie." Placing her arms around each of them, she snuggled them, kissing the tops of their heads.

CHAPTER 6

Lila

THE CHANGE FELT right. A new beginning of sorts. Different, but good. Even though Lila had gotten rid of many things before her move, there had still been a lot to unpack and she was thankful, Cara had spent all weekend with her setting up the new townhouse.

"Looks like we're down to the last box, Lila. It says 'Family' on the top."

"Family?" Looking puzzled, "Everything I packed was labelled with a room name, so I'd know where it goes."

"How about I make us some tea, Lila, while you do the honours of unpacking your final mystery box."

"Sounds like a plan. I'm looking forward to being done and putting my feet up, so a cup of tea sounds perfect."

As Cara made her way to the kitchen, Lila pulled open the folded flaps of the family box. Staring up at her was a picture of her mom. Instantly her heart kicked into overdrive like a race car's engine being revved with no let up. Falling back onto the couch, the memories flooded her thoughts, her body tensed, and her t-shirt dampened. The voice inside her head tried to talk herself down, but it wasn't working. Her breaths became erratic, and she started hyperventilating.

Cara came running over "My God Lila, are you okay?"

Lila closed her eyes. "My heart, it's beating so fast."

"What can I do? Do you want me to call an ambulance?"

"I think I just need a moment," bringing her hands up to her face and resting her elbows on her knees.

"Let me take you to the hospital, Lila. You should get checked out."

Lila looked away, "I think it might have been another panic attack."

"Another panic attack?"

"I think when we were driving back from spreading your parent's ashes, I had the first one."

"Wait, I thought you'd been upset then because we were talking about Robert."

"No, I'm pretty sure it was because we had been talking about your mom and my mom came to mind.

"I don't understand, Lila. Why would thinking about your mom cause you to have a panic attack?"

Taking in a huge deep breath, Lila crossed her arms in front of her chest. "I've never shared this part of my life with anyone Cara, not even Robert. Keeping it buried was easier than having to relive it, by talking about it. It's now affecting me physically though, so I think it's time to let it out"

Cara could see tears building in Lila's eyes.

"My mom wasn't always like this, Cara, but after my little sister died of Leukaemia when I was eleven, and my dad left the following year; moving out west somewhere to start up a business, it changed my Mom. She told me he left because he was unable to come to grips with my sister's death and being around us was a constant reminder of what he had lost. My mom's once sweet and caring disposition transformed into a very angry and hateful woman. My bedroom which used to be my happy place, a place where I'd had tea parties and played barbies, became a place of fear and horror. I could always tell from the look in her eyes that the rage was building. I knew how it would start and I knew how it would end. Even thinking about it now brings me right back to that time. I would hear her slippers clipping the bottom of her heels as she came up the stairs. I would brace for the tornado that was about to come ripping through my door. Just the sound of the knob turning, the click signifying the door was ajar, was enough to set my entire body into uncontrollable shakes. I would say repeatedly to myself, don't cry, don't cry, don't cry, but as soon as she began, the tears would come streaming down my cheeks. I'd look up at her and see her clenched teeth with the same question on her lips every time. *What the hell are you crying about? You've got nothing to cry about. Answer me. ANSWER ME!!!!!* I wanted to scream I hate you, leave me alone, but I didn't, and my silence angered her more. Her fists would start to pound my tiny frame. Through it all, I'd say to myself, *it'll stop, it'll soon stop.*"

Cara placed her hand on Lila's knee. Her heart was breaking for her friend.

"When she was spent, it was over. She would leave, slamming my door behind her. Through blurry wet eyes, I would look at the light from the hallway pushing through the small space at the bottom of my door, waiting, knowing it wouldn't be long and she would be back, back to hug me, saying how sorry she was for what she'd done. I hated that hug more than what she'd done. The hug wasn't for me, it was for her.

"Oh my God, Lila, I'm so sorry that happened to you."

"When I got the news that my mom had died of stage four cancer when I was twenty-five, all I felt was a relief. I hadn't seen her for years and all I could think was she's finally out of my life for good. I know that sounds terrible Cara, but it's exactly how I felt. She's the reason I never had kids and she's the reason I lost touch with my dad!"

Reaching out, Cara hugged Lila tight, wanting to take all her pain away. "I'm so sorry Lila." Releasing her hold, and looking into Lila's eyes, "Thank you for trusting me with this. Whatever you need, know I'm here for you."

"Thank you for listening, that's exactly what I needed."

"Promise me, Lila, you'll make a doctor's appointment just to make sure you're all good."

"I will, Cara. I promise."

CHAPTER 7

Angel

C ARA HAD BEEN going to Kids Play Place since Dani and Cody had been two and four. This evening, just like on many of their other visits, she was second-guessing her decision the minute she walked through the front door. The incessant dinging from the electronic games and the shrill squeals of excited children assaulted her ears as she dodged a mom beelining for the exit door with her toddler in tow, doing his utmost to release his wrist, screaming, "I don't want to go, I don't want to go!" as the doors closed behind them. If it weren't for her kids' love of this place, she would have stopped coming years ago.

While waiting for Dani and Cody to get their entry wristbands, Cara noticed a mother gathering all her stuff to leave. "Let's grab that table way over there, kids," Cara said.

Dani and Cody sprinted and then hovered, waiting for the lady to leave.

"Perfect timing," she said as she passed Cara with her kids.

Seated, her feet aching, Cara glanced around to see where the kids had dashed off to.

There *she* was.

Cara had seen her here often but had never spoken to her. She stood out among all the other mothers dressed in sweatpants and oversized T-shirts, with dried food stains and spit-up on their shoulders. Most of them looked frazzled trying to keep track of their older kids running amuck in the ball pits and climbing apparatus or from the constant motion of chasing their newly walking toddlers.

This woman was different. She stood out in her Dolce & Gabbana blouse, Nine jeans and Jimmy Choo shoes. Her effort was present and contemplated. She didn't walk; she glided past everyone, dangling her Coach purse at her elbow, palm faced upward, fingers bent at the knuckles so her perfectly manicured French-tipped nails could be seen on her petite, feminine hands. Cara could have sworn this woman grew as she crossed the room. She was attractive, but not a perfect-ten runway model type with legs that never stopped, as Cara didn't believe she broke five foot two. Today that glide was coming Cara's way.

"I can't find an empty table anywhere; would it be okay if I sat with you?"

"Um, yes, of course; please join me."

"I can't believe how busy it is in here tonight. Walmart must have closed early." She grinned arrogantly as she scanned the room. "I'm Angel Anwir, by the way. I've seen you here many times."

Cara's cheeks reddened with the knowledge that she had noticed her. "I'm Cara Munden. It's nice to meet you."

"I'm so glad you got a table, and I get to share it with you."

"Thank goodness that lady was leaving. I couldn't have stood while my kids played. I've been out all day viewing possible houses to live in, and I'm beat."

"I've had such a busy day too. So many meetings. I even made someone cry today."

"Really?" Cara was unsure what to make of that comment.

"You'd think people would act more professional at the office. One of my staff was away the last few days because she has a sick kid. I told her she didn't see me taking time off when my kids get sick." Leaning in close, winking, she said, "Well, not that she knows. Then she starts crying, telling me this big sob story like it's my problem. Some people are just so selfish."

Cara didn't feel comfortable and wanted to change the subject. "How old are your kids?"

"From my first marriage, I have a twenty-year-old son named Justin."

"Twenty! You look way too young to have a twenty-year-old." By Angel's flawless glowing skin, Cara had thought she was maybe thirty-five.

"Everyone tells me that! After I left him, I remarried and had two more kids. That's them over there, pointing to the monkey bars over a large ball pit. Ella is my oldest and Jayden is the little blonde one beside her. I don't know how much longer Ella is going to want to come to this place. She's almost a teenager and I pretty much drag her here now, but not Jayden, she loves it. I think Jayden would go anywhere I take her because she just wants to be wherever I am."

"She loves her momma."

"It can be a little stifling. It's hard for me to get my own space sometimes because most of the time she sticks to me like glue."

"Enjoy it while they still want to be around you, Angel. One day they'll be grown and off on their own. Hopefully, then they'll still want to make time for us."

"True, but I'm looking forward to that time."

Cara thought that comment too was a little strange. "Your girls look to be close in age to my kids. What school does Ella and Jayden go to?"

"St. Paul 11 in Okotoks."

"Mine too. I bet they all know each other."

"Where are you and your husband looking for your new home?"

"It's just my kids and me moving to a new place. We've been looking but haven't found the right one yet."

"Ah, so we have something in common, Cara. My divorce was finalized last month. It was quick and took only two months after I moved out. The happiest day of my life leaving that booze-hound behind! Can you believe alcohol was more important to him than I was? He was crazy. How long have you been divorced?"

"Well, we only split about two and a half months ago. We haven't done any official paperwork, not even a separation agreement. We're trying to do things as amicably as possible, especially for our kids, and if I'm being honest, the thought of being on my own scares me. That's a big reason we're all still living in the same house."

"No way, yikes!"

"I have a suite in the basement though, which helps, but I know it's not the best situation. Before the three of us leave, I want to have a good plan in place."

"Found our first difference, Cara. Three days after I told my ex I wasn't going to put up with any more of his insanity, the kids and I moved into a rental home."

"Really? I'm a plan A-B-C-D kind of gal."

"Not me, Cara. I'm more of a react-now-and-fly-by-the-seat-of-my-pants gal."

This caused both Cara and Angel to burst out laughing.

"Hey Cara, I'd only planned to drop in tonight for a short bit so the kids could burn off some steam. I've enjoyed getting to know you. Would you want to hang out again sometime? Maybe grab a drink?"

"Sure, let's do it. Here's my number."

Cara is exactly what I have been looking for. It's been three months, and I'm ready to have somebody back in my life. She's genuine and seems kind, qualities I wish I had. I wouldn't mind getting together with someone like her. She's tall and fit and I love her thick dark brown hair…those blue-green eyes, I'd like to swim in that ocean. I'm pretty sure she's straight, but even spaghetti's straight until it's wet. That doesn't mean I couldn't get her to fall for me. Heck, who wouldn't fall for all this?

CHAPTER 8

Jay

THE KNOCK STARTLED Cara. Like most evenings after she'd tucked the kids into their beds, she was downstairs on her couch watching Netflix, sipping her favourite Tim Hortons mint tea.

"Hey, Cara, do you have a moment to talk?"

"Yes, of course; come in."

Jay hesitated and instead leaned against the doorframe, his stature blocking most of the basement hall light from entering her room. "I want to tell you something instead of you hearing it from someone else."

Cara drew her knees up to her chest, wrapping her arms around them.

"I've found someone, and it's becoming more serious. I think it's time for you to find a home for yourself and the kids, a place you'll all be happy."

Jay's words should have hurt her, but they didn't; that boat had already sailed. Hearing what he had just said brought her a sense of relief. She no longer had to feel guilty for ending the relationship because he had found someone and would be fine. Letting go of the grip around her legs and exhaling, "I appreciate you having the guts to tell me yourself, Jay. Thank you for that. I have been looking for homes, but I haven't found anything that works, except for maybe the run-down house on the acreage fifteen minutes from here, the one I've been renovating for a flip investment. I've been wrestling with keeping it for the kids and me. It's so close to this place, making it easy for them to go back and forth between us, and since it's an acreage, the transition would be like what they've always lived in. I'm pretty sure I could have it completed in a couple of months."

"That sounds like a great idea, Cara. You should do that."

CHAPTER 9

Friends

Cara met Lila at the door to Caffe Beano with extended arms. Lila's hug was warm and comforting against the twenty-five-below-zero wind chill. Holding Cara out at arm's length, "You look amazing, Cara. I'm always impressed by how well you keep yourself together no matter what's going on in your life."

"With a compliment like that, Lila, coffee and dessert are on me today."

Scrambling to get out of the cold, Cara was immediately enveloped by the welcoming smells of freshly brewed coffee and baked goods, helping her instantly forget the freezing temperatures on the opposite side of the frosted glass door.

In her larger-than-life voice, Sophie belted out, "Yo chicas, over here!"

Cara looked at Lila, squinting and biting her lower lip. "Trust me, you'll love her! Cara had been friends with Sophie ever since their daughters started kindergarten together. After they had both dropped their kids off and walked out to the parking lot, Cara was the only other mom besides Sophie who wasn't teary-eyed or crying that their babies were now in school. Sophie noticing this, looked at Cara and blurted out, 'Hallelujah to freedom, let's grab a drink!' From that day forward, the two of them became friends. "Sophie, this is Lila; Lila, this is Sophie."

"Well fuck, Cara, you're right! She does look like Sandra Bullock."

Lila's cheeks grew pink. "I don't see it, but thanks for the compliment. It feels like I already know you, Sophie. Cara has shared many shenanigans that the two of you have gotten into. It's nice to meet the legend firsthand, finally."

"Good to know my reputation is expanding!" Sophie sported a cheeky, proud expression.

"I'll get the coffee so you guys can get to know each other better. Irish cream Americano for you?" She pointed at Lila. "And just straight black coffee for you? Correct?"

"Just like my men, Cara!" Sophie winked at Lila.

Walking to the counter and shaking her head, Cara could hear Sophie breaking into one of her stories. Cara felt truly blessed for her wonderful friends. With a tray of coffee and brownies, Cara made her way back to the table. "What lies are you telling Lila, Sophie?"

"Lies? Me?"

Just as Cara was about to sit down, a gust of cold air from the opened door blew in, causing her to shiver. Her nose crinkled as two teenagers sauntered by giggling, leaving traces of sweet skunk smell lingering.

"Now that reminds me of a Sophie story, ladies, and I use the word 'lady' lightly around you, my friend." Cara made direct eye contact with Sophie. "That party last year at your sister's. I was standing in the kitchen, Lila, when Sophie went barreling past me, stating she was off for a hoot in the backyard. Not even five minutes after she left the room, I heard pounding on the patio window. When I turned to see what all the commotion was about, there was Sophie, a smile on her face, shirt up, bare boobs squished against the glass, a nearly finished joint in her mouth and both hands in the air holding the rock-on pose. That's what you're getting into, Lila, with Sophie coming into your life."

"I love stories about me!" Sophie grinned ear to ear.

After stirring the cocoa powder topping into her coffee, Lila looked up. "Your call last week took me by surprise, Cara, but you seem okay with the news."

"I was surprised as fuck, too, Cara!" A group of Lulu lemon moms sneered at Sophie and then whispered amongst themselves. Sophie not missing a beat held her steaming cup of coffee up in the air, smiled directly at them and said, "Cheers to a fucking great day ladies," before bringing her attention back to the table saying, "Where were we?"

"I'm glad he told me, guys. Believe it or not, it makes me feel better knowing he has found someone and won't be alone when the kids and I move out. He's also made it easy for me to finally take the last step of moving out on my own."

Sophie huffed, "It never takes guys long to find a replacement. Women are like cars to them. When they don't work anymore, it's time to get another one."

"That does seem to be pretty common, Sophie. Hey, I need to share the cutest thing Cody said to me the other day. I swear he's such an old soul. I told both kids we would be moving soon and that I'd been struggling a little with doubts and fears about living alone because I'd never done that before. I lived with my parents until I graduated from university, and then I married their dad and moved in with him. With his big blue eyes barely visible through all his shaggy dirty blond hair, Cody looks up at me and says, 'Mom, you aren't going to be alone because you'll be with us.' The things out of that kid's mouth make me want to squeeze him till he pops!"

"He's just so sweet, Cara." Lila blew on her Americano.

"How long until the house is ready? We need to plan a housewarming party, maybe hire some strippers."

"It should be ready in about three more weeks. I've doubled up on the construction crew to get it done faster. Yes, to the party! No to the strippers, Sophie! Even though it is a little scary, I'm excited now to start this next chapter of my life."

"It blows me away how positive you are about it all, Cara. I love that about you, my friend." Just before Lila took a big bite of her brownie, she asked, "Anything else happening in your life?"

"I met a new friend at Kids Play Place."

"No surprise there, Miss Social Butterfly!" A mischievous smile spread across Sophie's face. "Did you meet in the ball pit?"

"Ha, ha, Sophie. You're so funny. She was there with her two kids, and we ended up sitting together because it was so busy. Ever since we've been meeting up each week for drinks. I think you guys would like her."

"Well, be sure to invite her to the housewarming party. Sophie and I will welcome her with open arms."

"Speak for yourself, Lila," Sophie said. "I'll need to meet her first."

CHAPTER 10

Angel

CARA SAT UP at the bar watching the bartender prepare her drink order while she waited for Angel to arrive. Pete's Place was a local pub that served great salt and pepper wings, cheap happy hour beer and a different band almost every evening. Hearing the front door open, Cara turned to see Angel walking in.

"Hello, Cara. Sorry, I'm late. Traffic was busy out there."

"No worries," getting up to hug her. "I'm just glad you're finally able to meet up again. I thought you weren't interested in hanging out anymore after cancelling last week and again this Monday." Cara had always had a three-chance rule when it came to friends. If she made the effort to invite someone out and, after three tries, the friend never got together with her, Cara stopped asking. She felt it wasn't worth it if she had to work that hard on a friendship.

"It's been a crazy couple of weeks, Cara. Work has been overwhelming, and I've had the worst migraine that just doesn't want to end."

"I'm sorry to hear that. Hopefully, those Coronas and China White shooters coming in our direction will wash your stresses and your headache away."

"I'll need a glass with that beer," Angel said to the server. As she walked back to get one, Angel leaned in close to Cara, "I'm not putting my lips on any bottle. Who knows how many dirty hands have touched the top? I nuke my library books before reading them for the same reason."

"Fair, um, I guess; I never looked at it that way. The Pub is hopping tonight, hey? Nothing better than a night out enjoying wings, drinks, and good company. This is a perfect evening for me."

"Besides hanging out with you, Cara, I rarely go out. I have one friend I see maybe once every two or three months. Normally after work, I like the quiet of home."

"Seriously, once every two or three months? I see my friends all the time."

"Let's order another round when she comes back with my glass, so we won't have to wait long for our next drink."

When the country band finally started their first song, Cara glanced at her watch only to realize they had already been there for over two hours.

"You're beautiful, Cara." Angel reached out and pushed a piece of Cara's hair behind her ear.

Like the last couple of times, they had hung out Angel was already tipsy. Her eyes always gave it away, working double time to focus when she talked to Cara.

"Do you think you will start dating once you move out?"

Cara sat back and thought about it. "It's been over twenty-four years since I've been on a date outside Jay." Cara had to let that thought sink in. "Honestly, I've been too busy getting the new house ready to even think about dating."

"Hmmm."

"Hey, so next weekend is the move-in date. I've told you about my two closest friends, Lila and Sophie. They thought I should have a ladies' night to celebrate the monumental occasion of living on my own. I looked at my calendar, and the kids will be with their dad the last weekend of this month. I was thinking of a hot tub party on Saturday the thirtieth at around six. Would you be available to come? I'm sure you'll love my friends."

"Sounds like fun; count me in."

⁂

I need to be more careful about cancelling my time with Cara. She didn't seem to like that too much. Not that it matters to me, but I'll stop doing that, at least for now. Since I'm going to meet her friends it's time to turn on the charm and win them over. I'm not too keen on social events; my insecurities heighten in those situations, but I'm good at keeping up a façade. I'll do whatever it takes, and I'll say whatever I need to say to make them like me. They'll like me. I always fool people into liking me.

CHAPTER 11

The Proposition

~~~

THAT SATURDAY EVENING was cold, the booze was flowing, and the laughs were nonstop.

Everyone was hitting it off and having a blast. Close to the firepit, trying to stay warm, Cara stood, holding her mittened hand out, beer bottle clasped tight, looking out at Lila, Sophie and Angel. "I'm so glad you all came tonight to celebrate the first of hopefully many parties at my new home."

"Woo hoo!" echoed throughout.

"I still think we should have ordered up some strippers," spilling red wine directly from the bottle onto her jacket as Sophie drove her hand up to the dark sky. "I guess the metal marshmallow poles will be the only things seeing some sticky action tonight!"

Cara giggled before turning on her heels and heading toward the house. "I'm freezing, guys. I'm getting in the hot tub."

Angel's head bobbed to each word as she said, "I'll join you." Succeeding on her second attempt to stand.

"Make sure she doesn't drown, Cara," Sophie chirped.

Angel clung to Cara's arm for dear life, doing her best not to fall over on the uneven snow-covered path.

"Sophie and I are going to stay and roast the last marshmallows, Cara," Lila said. "I'll tidy up before we join you guys in the tub. Hopefully, Sophie's provocative dance around the roasting stick will be over by then."

"One can only hope, Lila. Thanks for your help. You're the best!"

"I beg to differ!" Sophie hollered.

Lila never drank much, so Cara knew she could count on her to organize the firepit and Sophie. Cara's toes tingled in the welcoming heat as she submerged in the 103-degree water. She couldn't see Lila or Sophie through the rising steam, but she could hear their belly laughs echoing. The four rum and cokes she had consumed had her feeling a little fuzzy, but nowhere near the condition of Angel. Cara watched her come out through the patio doors and stumble toward the tub. "Be careful getting—"

Angel broke back up through the surface from the nosedive Cara witnessed as the word "in" left her mouth.

"Oh my gosh, are you okay?"

"I'm fine." Angel looked at Cara with googly eyes, hair plastered like a hockey helmet. Cara shut her eyes and leaned back against the cushioned headrest. Her calm passed instantly when her eyes bolted open from the warmth of a pair of lips pressed up against hers. Cara's hands automatically jumped to Angel's shoulders to prevent her from coming back for round two.

"Why can't we be more than just friends, Cara?"

It took Cara a few seconds to register what just happened... along with a couple more to process what Angel had said. Cara thought Angel must be even drunker than she looked. She peered out to see if Lila or Sophie had seen what just happened, knowing instantly the fog was far too thick for them to have seen.

"Let's be more than friends, Cara!" Angel's words sounded like her tongue was stuck to the bottom of her mouth.

"I think you've had one too many tonight, Angel. You and I are friends, and I would never want to ruin that."

Angel repositioned herself so she was sitting directly beside Cara, her leg now touching Cara's leg. Cara felt Angel's hand sliding up her inner thigh. Grabbing it, she stopped Angel from reaching the final destination just as Lila and Sophie came into view.

"What's up, *bitches?*" Sophie dropped her clothes on the spot and hopped in buck naked.

Cara caught Lila's inquisitive look as she went inside to get her bathing suit on.

CHAPTER 12

Is This Really Happening

Cara's entire being all week long had been riding a natural high. She wasn't sure why, but the center of her core felt as if it was glowing inside, filling her with overwhelming excitement. She had experienced something similar in the past when she'd hiked up the glacier at Lake Louise and once again in British Columbia when she was walking alongside a fast-moving brook in Nelson. The sensation always made her feel one with the world, a feeling she hadn't felt for a very long time. The weather was still pretty cold to do a long walk outside, so today, Lila, Sophie, and Angel were going to meet with Cara inside the Field-house, a new recreation centre built just on the outskirts of town to get a walk in on the running track. She was sure there would be many stories and laughs from last weekend's night of fun, so she wasn't surprised to see Sophie re-enacting the marshmallow pole dance as she approached the group. "Who needs strippers when you got a Sophie on your team, right!" Cara said.

"That's right, Cara, and you didn't even have to pay me."

Laughter broke out, with only Angel looking sheepishly away. After a warm hugging hello to Lila and Sophie, Cara said, "Bring it on in for a hug, Angel," just to let her know, without saying anything in front of the other two, that all was good between them.

"It feels like I've had a hangover all week."

Angel chimed in, "Me too, Sophie."

"I'm glad I don't drink like you two fish," Lila said.

Sophie swung her arm around Lila's shoulder, "Someone has to take care of us, Lila, and to be completely honest…" winking, "it's the only reason I told Cara you could be my friend."

An hour was just enough time for the stories to wind down and plans to be made for their next get-together. After hugging goodbye, Lila and Sophie walked out of the building and over to their cars at the far end of the lot, leaving Cara and Angel on their own.

"About last weekend, Angel. It's okay if you're into women; it's no big deal."

Angel looked directly into Cara's eyes. "I'm not just into any women, Cara. I'm into you."

Her words froze Cara in place. She had thought Angel's forwardness on the weekend was due to her drunken state, but now, that didn't seem to be the case. Cara had never thought about Angel or any woman in that way. All Cara could muster before leaving the building was, "Ah, see you next week, Angel."

You're the one I would call, Mom, if something crazy like this was happening. Is she actually into me? She's my friend, and I'm not into women. I'm trying to imagine what you would say to me, Mom, if I came to you with this. You'd probably have said, 'Cara, you might have handled your reply to Angel a little better.' Giggling to herself, Cara just shook her head. *She caught me by complete surprise, Mom. I had no idea what to say.*

CHAPTER 13

Lila

Sitting in the waiting room Cara looked over at Lila, "I know I harped on you about getting in to see your doctor due to the panic attacks, Lila but I'm glad you finally did. It's great she put you through a barrage of tests over the last couple of weeks, so hopefully today we should finally get some answers as to why you just haven't been yourself lately. Let's hope it's nothing, but better safe than sorry."

"I've been trying to stay positive while waiting for the results, but having the follow-up at the hospital, instead of my family doctor's office isn't making me feel very confident."

"Whatever it turns out to be, Lila, we'll get through it together."

They both jumped in unison to the door opening.

"I'm Dr. Munro, head of Oncology. You are?"

"I'm Lila and this is my friend Cara. I was expecting to see my family doctor today."

"Dr. Kass thought it best if we met instead. We found something in your test results that needs to be dealt with right away."

Cara reached out for Lila's hand. It was clammy.

"It's a good thing you came in for tests when you did, Miss Alstead."

"You can call me, Lila."

"Okay, Lila. I'm not going to beat around the bush. Your results showed well-differentiated tumours on your thyroid called Papillary thyroid cancer. We caught it early enough that your percentages are high for a full recovery with surgery. No chemo or radiation should be needed. We want to do the surgery as quickly as possible, so I've scheduled you, three days from now on Monday, March 11th at 8:30 am. We will be removing your thyroid. We're hopeful that there hasn't been any spread to the lymph nodes but if we see anything, we will remove those areas too. Do you have any questions?"

When Dr. Munro stopped talking, Cara looked at Lila and saw nothing but a glazed look across her face. Taking the lead, Cara asked, "What should we expect regarding recovery time?"

"Most people return home the day after surgery, but if you're working Miss Alstead, it would be a good idea to take a couple weeks off to give yourself a good amount of time to recover. You will need to refrain from any heavy lifting or anything that may cause strain to your neck for up to three weeks following surgery."

Lila just sat there looking pale.

"Will Lila be on any meds?"

"Yes, she will need to take a thyroid hormone pill called Levothyroxine to replace the natural hormone she will no longer produce on her own. This pill will help with maintaining normal metabolism and possibly lower the risk of the cancer coming back."

"This is a lot to take in Dr. Munro, but I'll make sure Lila is here Monday morning. Thank you for meeting with us and for explaining everything."

"The good news is we've caught it early and it's a curable cancer."

CHAPTER 14

Feelings Are Forming

Today was warm enough for Cara to crack open her living room windows, letting in the late May spring air. She had just finished preparing the charcuterie boards with a variety of meats, cheeses, crackers, and olives she had picked up from Safeway that morning. After a little back and forth in her mind, she decided to display the snacks on the island instead of the dining table for a less formal feel. Just as she dropped the last of the ice cubes into the jug of sangria, she heard vehicles pulling in on her gravel driveway. A huge smile spread across Cara's face as she met Lila, Sophie and Angel, at the front door. "Well hello, ladies. Perfect timing. I'm all ready for you."

Lila hugged Cara before taking off her shoes and making her way into the kitchen. Cara noted that even with the warmer temperatures, Lila was wearing a turtleneck. Cara thought she must still be feeling a little conscientious about the surgery scar. Lila announced, "This spread looks amazing, Cara. You shouldn't have gone to all this trouble."

"Sure, she should have," Sophie said, as she high-fived Cara and made a beeline to the Sangria jug.

Angel took her time removing her shoes and when she had finished, she also took her time hugging Cara, holding on much longer than Lila had, allowing Cara to inhale the intoxicating smell of Angel's perfume. Cara's heart raced as Angel's gaze lingered after their embrace.

It was Sophie's voice, that rallied Cara back. "Okay, Cara, since you're our fearless leader, what's the plan for next weekend's girl's getaway to Canmore?"

Taking a second to regroup her thoughts, Cara filled everyone in. "Through AirBnB, I found a four-bedroom Chalet with two bedrooms up and two down with a bathroom on each floor. There are amazing views of the Three Sisters Mountains off the back deck and wait for it, there's a hot tub!"

"Yes, shouted Sophie", clinging everyone's glasses even if there wasn't a drink in them.

"It's close to town so we should be able to walk everywhere. The cost for the accommodation works out to be a hundred and fifty bucks each and I was thinking we can just stop at a grocery store in town before checking in and we'll just split that bill."

Lila was the first to say, "Thanks for organizing everything, Cara," with Sophie and Angel right behind her.

"It was my pleasure, ladies." Raising her now-filled glass in the air, "I want to make a toast to Lila. We all couldn't be happier that your surgery went well and that you're now feeling so much better and can join us next weekend."

Everyone sang out. "Cheers to Lila"

When Cara glanced around the island she caught Angel gazing at her. Ever since the hot tub party, Cara's feelings towards Angel had shifted. For some reason, with each new get-together, something was percolating. With each look, feelings at least for Cara, were intensifying. Neither had said a word to the other after what had been said or done, but with every interaction between them, something was growing. Cara couldn't quite understand why she was becoming attracted to Angel or even open to such a possibility, but she couldn't stop the feeling of being drawn to her.

Out of nowhere, Sophie shouted out, "I feel it's only right to disclose that I snore,"

"Well, if that's the case, let's put her in one of the basement bedrooms, preferably the furthest room from me." Giggled Angel.

"Ouch, a dagger to my heart." Sophie made a motion as if she'd just been stabbed, causing everyone to chuckle.

"Thanks for telling us, Sophie. I'll figure out the sleeping arrangements and let you all know. Why don't we all meet back here after work next Friday around six and drive up in my truck? That way we're all in one vehicle." Everyone around the island raised their glasses in agreement.

Cara *can't stop looking at me and I love the attention. I knew I could get her to fall for me.*

CHAPTER 15

Pandoras Box

"THANK FUCK, WE'RE finally here. I wasn't sure if I was going to make it through the workweek. Two days and nights of fun in Canmore. I'm lining up tequila shots. Who's in?"

Cara, Lila, and Angel popped their hands into the air.

Upon arrival at their chalet, Cara shared with Sophie and Lila that they would be sleeping in the downstairs bedrooms, with her and Angel taking the two upstairs.

Lila asked, with one eyebrow raised, "Are you sure that's wise, Cara?"

Cara wondered if Lila had caught on to her plan. She erased the thought immediately. "I know you, Lila, and I can almost guarantee that you brought earplugs. Right?"

"Sure did! From our meetup last week, we all learned that the lovely Miss Sophie snores like a chainsaw."

"Hey, no judgment, guys. You should all be thankful I shared that with you." A cheeky smile on her face, dancing around the room with the tequila bottle taking a little swig each time she refilled anyone's shot glass.

"I knew you'd come prepared, Lila, and that's why I put you downstairs with Sophie." Was she imagining it, or was that a slight smile on Angel's face?

Cara grabbed her luggage and searched for her Bluetooth speaker. Finding it she took a moment to sync her phone and hit play on Deaf Leopard's song, 'Pour Some Sugar on Me.'

"Crank it up." Yelled Sophie, dropping her clothes right there and sprinting to the hot tub singing at the top of her lungs, "Pour some sugar on me, in the name of love."

Cara, Lila and Angel burst out laughing, before grabbing their bags and heading to their rooms to get changed into their swimsuits.

Cara and Angel nearly knocked each other over coming out of their rooms.

"You look smoking hot, in that bikini, Cara."

"Thanks, Angel!" She could feel her face going red without even looking in a mirror.

Walking behind Angel on their way to the hot tub, Cara couldn't push away the feelings of being sexually aroused. Was it the booze? Or was she seriously falling for Angel? "I'll see you in the tub Angel. I'm going to grab a few beers in an ice bucket for everyone."

Laughter and solving all the world's problems finished close to 2 a.m. Everyone was pretty liquored and ready to head back to their rooms for the night.

Cara left her bedroom door open, hoping that when Angel came out of the bathroom, she would notice it and come in. As Cara lay in the darkness, she saw Angel hesitate slightly outside her bedroom door before proceeding into her room directly across the hall.

Cara listened intently for the sound of Angel's door closing. The light went out, but the door stayed open. As she lay there, the pane of glass in her bedroom window rattled from the gusts of wind bouncing off the chalet while tree shadows eerily danced across her ceiling. Should she get up and go see Angel? Or maybe she should invite her to come over and talk?

Out of the darkness, she heard, "Do I make you nervous, Cara?"

Her heart felt like it had just jumped out of her chest to Angel's words. Was Angel making the first move? "No, you don't make me nervous."

"Can I come over and lay down with you? I won't do anything."

Cara thought to herself, *"It's not you I'm worried about doing something..."*

Angel's silhouette appeared in Cara's doorway. She watched as Angel seductively walked toward her bed, lifted her blanket, and slid in beside her. Angel was so close that her hair tickled Cara's nose, and Cara wondered if Angel could feel her heartbeat pounding against her back as Cara couldn't recall it ever beating this hard.

As Angel adjusted her position, the scent of her cherry blossom body spray wafted, causing every hair on Cara's body to rise. She wanted to gently move Angel's hair from her shoulders and place soft kisses behind her neck and ear. She yearned to inch her fingertips down her arm, so their hands could clasp, and she could pull Angel in tight. Cara's body ached to press up against her. Would Angel press back? Would she want Cara to touch her?

Cara's mind started to swirl. She knew the door to the bedroom was still open. What if Lila or Sophie were to see them? How would she explain this? Even though every fibre in her being wanted to follow through on her thoughts, doubt flooded her mind. She shouldn't be doing this. What was she doing? Panicking Cara jumped out of the bed, saying, "I can't do this, Angel." She walked over to Angel's bedroom and closed the door.

The next morning, Cara lay restless, tangled in her sheets. She had spent almost the entire night going over and over how to explain herself to Angel. She'd wanted to be with her last night, but her anxious thoughts had gotten the best of her. With her room brightening from the morning sun, it was important for Cara to talk with Angel before Lila and Sophie came upstairs.

She found Angel lying quietly awake on her back. Sitting down, her hip nestled tight into Angel's waist, she placed her hands on Angel's, which were resting across her stomach. "I'm so sorry for how I reacted last night. I panicked! I didn't know how to explain our situation if Lila or Sophie saw us together. I want you to know I have some unexplainable feelings for you and had hoped to share them with you last night, but I just freaked out. It was wrong of me to jump up and leave without an explanation to you. I'm very sorry for acting that way."

"Don't worry about it, Cara. Over the last few months, I've constantly been thinking about you. We could be perfect together. We are both on our own; instead of being alone, we could have each other."

Those words were music to Cara's ears. Knowing someone was thinking about her and choosing her felt incredible. "We're all good then? We can forget about how I acted last night?"

Angel looked at Cara with the biggest smile and said, "Yes, we're all good."

The relief had Cara expressing a big sigh. "I would like to try again tonight. Are you up for that?"

With a devilish look in her dark brown eyes, Angel said, "Yes, most definitely."

After cooking up and eating a huge breakfast of pancakes, bacon, sausage and toast, everyone took turns in the bathroom getting ready so they could head out for an afternoon hike. It was a gorgeous day with blue skies and little clouds. The temperature was perfect for hiking at sixteen degrees. The four of them made their way in a line along the Bow River that flowed right through the town with Angel leading the pack, followed by Cara right behind her, Sophie then Lila.

Cara couldn't stop herself from looking at Angel's bare-toned legs in her patterned black and grey Lulu lemon shorts, her butt jiggling ever so slightly with each step. The sexual tension built as each minute passed. Once in a while, Angel would look back at Cara with a little smile that melted Cara's heart. Each look now meant something completely different.

"Cara! Hey, Cara." It was the tap on her shoulder from Sophie that brought her back.

"What? Sorry, Sophie. I was daydreaming."

"We're almost back down the mountain. Lila and I were just saying, we could eat. How about you?"

"I am getting pretty hungry. How about you Angel? Are you hungry?

Angel turned looking directly at Cara. "I could eat just about anything right now." Licking her lips and biting her lower lip.

Cara swallowed hard and couldn't wait for nighttime to arrive.

Everyone had settled in their rooms early from being so tired from the day's hike. As soon as it was quiet, Cara entered Angel's room and locked the door. Unable to hold back any longer, she went in for a kiss. The softness of Angel's lips, followed by the taste of her tongue, had fireworks exploding within Cara. It didn't feel weird or wrong. It felt completely natural and so right.

Cara let her senses take over, falling into the moment. She repositioned herself so she lay next to Angel; soft kisses between them became more profound and passionate. The attraction she felt toward Angel was off the charts. She moved her body on top, and a rhythm took hold. The heat she felt was like being too close to a fire but not wanting to back away, the flames enticing her to stay as the dance progressed. The intensity continued to build. Cara's mouth moved from Angel's lips to her neck. Angel's pelvis began to move against Cara, showing her clear signs that she was on the right track. Cara's hands went into autopilot, lifting Angel's tank top and exposing her erect, beckoning nipples. Cara's mouth dropped onto them one at a time, giving each equal attention. Angel's hands held her there, letting her know she wanted everything Cara was giving. Soft moans escaped Angel as Cara's left palm slid past Angel's belly button.

That night, Pandora's box was opened.

CHAPTER 16

Lila

"Waiting is the worst, Cara. Look at that lineup of people. The hospitals are so short-staffed, and it's the patients who pay the price. Even when you have an appointment, you're still kept waiting."

Cara could see how stressful all this was on Lila. It was their second follow-up appointment since the surgery. Even though Dr. Munro, was confident he'd gotten all the cancer out, Lila still had to have regular follow-up visits to the hospital for the first year and it was breaking Cara's heart to see her friend holding on to so much worry at each appointment.

In the far corner of the waiting room, a little boy was crying as he held his left arm up to his mom, she doing her best to console him.

"Dr. Misner can you please report to Emergency, Dr. Misner emergency room please", muffled over the intercom.

"I really can't handle all this noise right now, Cara. It's going to be a while before I get in, so I'm going to go grab a quick snack from the vending machine we passed on our way in. Do you want anything?"

"I'm good, but thanks."

Lila hurried out making her way briskly down the corridor, careful to scoot out of the way of getting knocked down by a gurney being pushed by two EMTs towards the emergency room. Seeing an orderly coming in her direction, she asked, "I'm pretty sure I saw a vending machine on my way in, am I getting close?"

"You're almost there. Take your next right and you'll run right into it. You might have to wait a minute as I just saw the vending guy filling it when I walked by. It didn't look like he had too many boxes of snacks left to unload, so hopefully you won't have to wait too long."

"Appreciate it, thanks."

As Lila rounded the corner, she stopped and waited, watching the man from behind fill in the last of the missing chip bags. As he closed and locked the front glass, she could see that there were both Kit Kat bars and salt & vinegar chips available, so her trip was not wasted.

Turning to face Lila, the man smiled exposing a gap between his front teeth. "Sorry if I've kept you waiting Miss. She's all filled up and ready for you," reaching down to grab the empty boxes strewn in front of the machine.

Lila froze!

"I'm going to leave you my business card. I've received a few complaints lately with this machine, so if you have any issues, please don't hesitate to call the number on the card."

Lila watched him in silence as he walked down the hallway, boxes in hand. Eyeing the business card she saw his name in bold lettering…Jason Alstead.

"Paging Lila Alstead, Paging Lila Alstead!" Cara called out smiling as she walked passed him toward Lila. "They just called your name my friend. I told them I'd come find you and bring you right back."

Lila saw him stop in his tracks, turn in slow motion, eyes the size of saucers locking into hers, mouthing. "Lila?"

When they were on their way out of the hospital parking lot, Cara couldn't contain her thoughts any longer. "Oh my God Lila, that was insane. I couldn't be happier about your fantastic test results, but running into your Dad has to be one of the craziest things that's ever happened…ever! What are the odds that the two of you would run into each other? Like a billion to one?"

"Maybe even a trillion to one but I knew it was him as soon as he faced me and smiled. Except for the grey splattered throughout his hair, he looks like the picture I keep in my wallet." Sifting through the bill holder section, Lila pulled it out and showed it to Cara.

"It's blowing me away, Lila."

"The day I moved out at eighteen, I rummaged through my mom's closet looking for a picture of him. I was about to give up when I came across a shoe box buried in the back corner under a duffle bag. It was filled with family pictures and a bunch of unopened letters. I only had enough time to grab this picture because my mom came home early that day not feeling well. This picture has been in my wallet ever since."

"When was the last time he saw you?"

"I was twelve when he left."

Reaching over to hold Lila's hand, "This has got to be a lot for you to process."

"It's so surreal, Cara. I used to imagine walking into a Mercedes dealership and he was the salesman, dressed to the nine's in a fine tailored suit, or walking into a grocery store to see his face up on the wall under the manager's sign."

Cara distracted by Lila's story, slammed on the brakes just in time to prevent running a red light. "Yikes, sorry about that!"

"He told me he'd like to get together for a coffee and talk."

"How do you feel about that?"

"He's had well over twenty years to invite me for a coffee to talk. What could he possibly say to make up for what he's done? What do you think, Cara? Should I meet up with him?

"Oh, Lila, it's not my place to answer that for you. Just know that whether you choose to see him or not, I'll support whatever decision you make."

Lila sat on the black metal chair of Cafe Beano's patio, thankful for the awning above to protect her from the sun's blazing glare. The thermometer by the window showed twenty-nine degrees, so the sweat dripping down her body could easily be blamed on the early July heat and not her nerves. She had played out this exact moment over and over the past couple of weeks, but now that it was here, feelings of joy sat face to face with feelings of anger.

"Hello, Lila. May I join you?"

She pointed to the chair across from her as she couldn't quite form any tangible words to her Dad.

"Thank you for agreeing to meet with me."

Giving him a half-hearted smile, Lila squirmed a little in her chair.

"I want to start by saying, I'm so sorry, Lila. I'm sorry that it took me this long to make this day happen and I'm sorry for all the lost time that my actions cost us."

Words had escaped, Lila, but not her tears; they flowed like a rushing waterfall.

Reaching across the table holding out his hands to her, "I can't change the past, Lila, but I'm here now and I would be forever grateful if you allowed me to be part of your life."

Lila removed her hands from below the table and placed them in her daddy's hands. His touch felt comforting and safe. "Why did you leave and not come back for me?"

His Adam's apple heaved up and then dropped hard. "Lila, the death of your sister turned my world upside down, as I'm sure it did yours. Back then you were so young and because of that your Mother and I didn't share everything that was going on. I'd lost my job from missing so much work and no matter how hard I tried to move forward, there were just too many bone-crushing memories every time I stepped foot in our home. Everything reminded me of your sister and what I had lost. I know now, that what I did was not fair to you or your mother, but I needed to get away. I needed a fresh start in a new city, with a new home and a new job. The plan was always that you and your mother would join me as soon as you had finished seventh grade that year. We didn't want to upheave your life any more than it already was by moving you away from your friends halfway through the school year, so I moved out here and got everything set up for us."

"Then why didn't that happen and why didn't you ever get in touch?"

"I wrote you letters weekly, Lila."

"Mom never gave them to me."

"I called your Mother often, but as the months passed, each time I asked to speak with you, she said you were busy. She told me she thought the two of you were better off without me and that she had decided she was going to stay in Thunder Bay with you. I tried everything to convince her to come but all that did was anger her to the point where she stopped answering my calls altogether."

"Mom always gave me the impression that it was you who just left us."

"I will never forgive myself, Lila, for not trying harder. Maybe today can be a fresh start for you and me. I'm willing to do anything for a chance to make up for all the hurt I've caused you."

CHAPTER 17

Falling Hard

The pile of paperwork was a quarter of its height from this morning. Cara took in a deep breath and slowly let it out, feeling tired but also very satisfied with how productive her workday had been. Glancing out the office window, the sun looked like a candlelight ready to be blown out at the top of a willowy evergreen tree. Seeing the colourful flowers in her garden standing out against all the rich green grass brought her a feeling of personal joy.

Leaning back in her cushy black leather office chair, closing her eyes to relieve some of the day's strain, she thought about her mom and how she wished she was still around to have someone to talk to about Angel. If only she and Angel hadn't decided to keep it all a secret, she could have opened up to Lila. But with Lila's health scare and her dad back in her life, this probably wasn't the best time anyway to drop the huge newsflash. *I think for now, I'm actually okay with it being a secret. What if I opened up and it cost me my friendships? What if my kids don't understand? I'm not willing to chance any of that at this time.*

When Cara had spare time like this, her mind always turned to thoughts of Angel. Waking up or going to sleep, Angel danced throughout her mind. Cara was falling like she had never fallen before and even though it scared and sometimes confused her, there was nothing she wanted more. She knew 100 percent how strongly her feelings had been growing for Angel, but in the same breath, she wasn't always sure if Angel felt the same way. Angel would say things to Cara that made her want to believe Angel was feeling the same way, telling Cara often how much she missed her and that she couldn't wait to see her next, but even so, her actions didn't always align with her words. Cara's phone ring snapped her eyes open.

"Hello, this is Cara."

"Well, hello, Cara. This is your girlfriend, Angel."

A smile spread across Cara's face from the word 'girlfriend'.

"I was hoping you're free tomorrow so we can meet up and spend some time together."

"I would love that," bolting to a sit-up straight position. "Will it be just you and me?" Her excitement was clearly announced in the question. Cara hoped that would be the case because she was becoming frustrated with how often Angel would bring someone along when it was supposed to be just the two of them. It happened last week when she was to meet up with just Angel at her house, but when she arrived Angel's sister Liz was there. The week prior, they were supposed to meet for a walk, but when Cara arrived, Angel's daughter tagged along.

"Yes, I want to spend some time with just you."

"Count me in then. I can't wait to see you." When the call ended, Cara realized she jumped at every opportunity to spend time with Angel. All Angel had to do was ask and Cara would be there.

Her phone ring distracted her once again.

"Hello, this is Cara."

"Hello, this is Lila."

Cara giggled. "What's up?"

"I want to plan a dinner for you and me at my place."

"Well, I would love for you to plan a dinner for me," chuckling, "but what's the occasion?"

"You've been my rock through everything, Cara. My move, my cancer scare, all the doctor's appointments and always being a listening ear for me when it comes to my Dad. I honestly don't think I would've gotten through any of it without you. The least I can do is cook a nice meal for you."

"Well if I have to eat one of your great meals then I guess I have to!"

Lila laughed. "I remembered you saying you were organizing something for Angel's birthday coming up next week, so I didn't want to double-book us."

"That's very thoughtful to check on the date. I was planning to book the dinner on her actual birthday day, August 7th. She loves Sushi, so I thought we could all meet after work around six at the Sushi Grill over in Shaughnessy."

"Let me just check my calendar. Yup, that works for me. "Oops, I've got to run, Cara. The timer just went off on the stove. I'm making myself a mini roast with baked potatoes for supper. I'll text you later with some dates for our dinner date."

"Looking forward to it, Lila. Your meal sounds delicious. Enjoy!" Hanging up, Cara tapped her keyboard to bring the screen to life. She would take these next couple hours to write the poem that had been swimming in her mind as a birthday gift for Angel.

***

The birthday night had arrived. Cara sat patiently in her car waiting a few rows back from the restaurant entrance to catch Angel before she went in. She had seen Lila five minutes earlier, followed shortly after by Sophie. The parking lot on this side of the strip mall was always quite busy due to the movie theatre on the corner, and tonight was no different. As she watched the various cars drive around for the second and sometimes third time looking for an open parking spot, she finally noticed Angel drive by. When she had parked and was making her way toward the restaurant, Cara called out her name and waved her over to join her in her vehicle.

"Happy birthday, Angel!" Cara said when Angel sat in the passenger seat. Cara's embrace was all-encompassing; she hoped Angel felt the love radiating from every inch of her. "Instead of buying you something for your birthday, I wrote you a poem. It's not something I can give you in front of everyone else, so I wanted to give it to you here before we go in."

Angel's bottom lip went into a pout with a little "Aww" escaping her lips. She carefully slid off the deep purple ribbon that had kept the opaque scroll rolled tight. The paper Cara had chosen to house her heartfelt words had soft purple flowers, Angel's favourite colour, embedded within the sheet. The delicate paper held all of Cara's feelings she had been thinking about.

ONE DAY

> Our journey, where will it take us, where will it end
> The love that I've found so hard to comprehend
> We're both searching for something is it you, is it me
> Only time will tell if it's meant to be
> We shared our thoughts, and let our bodies be explored
> We crossed that line, we walked through that door
> What I feel for you, I have not felt for so long
> I yearned for this feeling and now it is strong
> I lost someone special, so close to my heart
> You filled the hole, so I would not break apart

Our friendship isn't anything, I have experienced before
The happiness it brings fills me right to my core
This new love that is growing sometimes feels out of control
As I try to figure out, the right way to go
I trust you like, I have never trusted before
I've put my faith in your hands, and I have released my control
The love that I am feeling, feels so true
I am not willing to let go, what I've started with you
Your smile, your eyes, it's all that I see
When I hold you in my arms, I finally feel free

A song I have found reminds me of you
I share it, hoping you feel it too
I know what we have, is finally true
You feel for me, the way I feel for you
Hearing your voice brightens my day
Texting my thoughts makes everything okay
When you're not around, I miss you so much
It makes me long for your gentle touch
If I had my way, I'd spend every moment with you
Maybe one day, my wish will come true

I love how you show me, in your own special way
That your feelings for me, are growing with each passing day
The chance I've taken, I hold no regrets
For what I have gained, I will never forget
I now feel secure, in what I have found
The doubts are gone, and I know my feelings are sound
I don't really know, what our futures hold
But I pray you're by my side, as I grow old

Our time alone is ever so rare
To show my feelings, I can rarely bear
But in my mind, my true thoughts come alive

I am able to show you, how I feel deep inside
Holding your hand, our fingers intertwined, hoping one day that you will be mine
I kiss your neck with the softest touch, my lips meet yours, and it's almost too much
I pull your body close to mine, and I know it's only a matter of time
I want to please you, and let you know, exactly how I feel
I want you to know that my love for you is real

ONE DAY we will be ready, and everything will be in place
No longer will we need to hide, our love we will embrace
I look forward to that day when it is YOU and ME
For then I will no longer wonder if it's meant to be

"Thank you, Cara, for such a beautiful gift." Placing her hands on either side of Cara's face, looking deep into her eyes, Angel said, "I love you, Cara."

Angel's words had Cara hugging her, wanting to hold on to the moment for as long as possible. Those three words had not been said out loud, and Angel was saying them to her. Cara was on cloud nine. "I love you too, Angel."

As they sat back, Angel blurted, "Before we go in, I need to share something with you."

"What is it?"

"I let my sister Liz know you and I are together."

Cara looked at Angel deer-like. They hadn't discussed telling anyone just yet.

"The first thing out of my sister's mouth was, 'Cara's going to get hurt,' but then she said how happy she was for me and that she was very supportive of us."

Cara couldn't believe the first person to learn about the two of them was okay with their choice. Maybe what they were trying to build with one another could work. *Why would Liz say I'm going to get hurt? Angel would never hurt me, she loves me.* Getting out of the truck and walking toward the restaurant, Cara floated across the parking lot, prouder than a peacock, that she was walking through the front door with this beautiful woman by her side.

CHAPTER 18

Greatest Fear Shared

"Stop all that barking and let Cara come in the house."

"How does so much noise come out of two such tiny dogs, Angel?"

"I wonder that myself all the time." Glaring down at them playing tug of war over a knotted-up chewy toy.

If Cara had to choose, she would have preferred that their weekends together were at her place instead of Angel's. Even though she loved dogs, Angels were so yappy and to make things worse they shed enough daily fur throughout the house to make sweaters for a lifetime. The floors weren't the only place assaulted; Angel's fabric furniture had to be carefully inspected before ever sitting down; otherwise, the lint brush, kept handy on the couch end table, would be needed. Cara used to joke with Angel that Swiffer products had to be her best friend.

"Whose car is that in your driveway, Angel?"

"It's mine. I bought it yesterday."

"I didn't know anything was wrong with your old one."

"There wasn't; it was a spur-of-the-moment purchase. I was driving by a Mercedes dealership on Wednesday and felt like I deserved a new vehicle…I really can't afford it but driving that car makes me feel like a million bucks."

"Well, I'm sure you look fabulous behind the wheel of that gorgeous burgundy car."

"Thanks, Cara. Did you want a cup of tea?"

"Yes, please!" Making her way over to one of the wooden stools at the island, Cara glanced around the kitchen. Whenever she was at Angel's, odd cupboard doors were left ajar, and it was rare to see her sink without dirty dishes in it, even though she owned a dishwasher. Angel's counters always had stuff on them. Whether it was cups left from previous morning coffees, breakfast dishes, or a pile of bills and receipts waiting to be filed, Cara always had to move a few things around, so they had a clean surface to share a tea. Cara prided herself on a clean home. She liked things to look tidy and organized; if she took something out of a cupboard or closet, she always put it back. Everything had its place in her mind, and taking the time to put things away right after she used them saved her from spending her weekends or free time doing major cleanups. Angel was not cut from the same cloth, but Cara could easily overlook that because she was in love with Angel, not her housekeeping skills.

"Cara, I'm so glad we're spending every second weekend together when our kids are with their dads! It's the best decision we've made together. I love waking up next to you. I love spending our mornings together talking and laughing, and most of all, I love our playtime…even before I grab my first morning coffee."

Cara's heart fluttered.

"I've never fallen for anyone like I've fallen for you, Cara! You're everything I've been looking for, and when I'm with you,

you make me feel so safe! In my past relationships, when things got bad, no one fought for me; they didn't try to win me back. I know you'd always fight for me."

"Of course, I will, Angel. You mean everything to me."

"I want you to know, Cara, that I notice all the special things you do for me. Like when you surprise me with flowers or send sweet texts. You know my love language, so nothing beats you going to my place on a Friday afternoon to tidy things up so I can have a relaxing weekend after a busy work week. I love it when you do that."

"I never mind doing those things for you! I want you to know how important you are to me, and that I'll always be there for you. You have no idea how much it's meant to me to spend these weekends together. Having those four days each month makes me feel connected with you, and it's what makes me feel I'm important to you because you're making time for me. These weekends together are what will help us grow as a couple. Also, just so you know I do miss you when we are not together."

"Ah," Angel said sporting her pouting lip. "Well, maybe we can also see each other on some of my flex Mondays. I'm getting them every second week now. You could come to my place after our kids are at school and have Monday morning playtime!"

"That sounds amazing. Count me in!"

"That reminds me, the key on the counter over there is for you. It's for my place so you can let yourself in on our special days."

Cara couldn't believe Angel was giving her a key. *She must see a future with me if she's giving me a key to her home. She wouldn't give me a key if she wasn't happy being in a relationship with me.* "Thanks, Angel. It means a lot that you feel safe enough with me to give me a key to your place. I'll be sure to give you a key to my place too. Hey, all this talk about keys for playtime…wanna?"

"Yes, but first I need to hang up some clothes I left on my bed." Causing them both to giggle.

"Um, I'm still vibrating over here." Her belly spasmed up and down from the orgasm shock wave. Turning to gaze at Angel's naked body, she ran her hand across her silky-smooth skin. How exciting it was to see Angel's body react to her gentle touch. "God you're beautiful."

Angel looked at her, smiled and kissed her deeply.

"Hey, if you could travel to one special place with me, where would you want to go?"

"I would like to go to San Diego with you, Cara! We'll probably never get an opportunity to go on a trip together, but I would love to go there with you."

"We're going one day, Angel, I promise!"

"What scares you the most in life, Cara?"

"Being alone," hurtled from Cara's mouth without hesitation.

"When we aren't a secret, and everyone knows we're a couple, we could be like this all the time, Cara, and we could live together when our kids are all grown up. You'd never be alone again!"

"What a beautiful thought. I would love that!"

"Hey, what should we do for our next weekend together?"

"You know what would be fun."

"What?"

"We could take the hour-long drive out to Canmore to go for a hike in the mountains or drive just a little farther to Banff and grab some of those yummy chocolate, caramel and nut bear paws from the chocolate store."

"That sounds like fun. We could even grab a beaver tail donut. I love the ones spread thick with Nutella and sprinkled with M&M's. Maybe I could pack us a little picnic basket with a bottle of my favourite pinot noir wine."

"That all sounds great and if we decide not to go for a drive, there's lots to do right here in Calgary. We could go downtown and take a long walk all along the Bow River. There are miles of walking paths with so many unique bridges to cross. Have you seen the new Peace Bridge? It's funky looking, but it's growing on me."

"I've only seen pictures, but I would love to check it out with you. Liz says there are tons of great bars and restaurants in the downtown core. She said downtown Calgary is changing from a work-only place, then straight back to the burbs, to a much more fun, hip place to hang out after the workday. Maybe that's where we could live one day, Cara."

"Wouldn't that be amazing!"

CHAPTER 19

Lila

C ARA ALWAYS FELT like she was walking into a showroom or a magazine spread whenever she entered a home of Lila's. She had a flair when it came to design. Walking over the dark wide plank floors, past the white leather couches filled with colourful textured pillows, Cara was in awe of the creativity that oozed from her best friend.

"My God, Lila, you have not lost your knack! I thought your place in Thunder Bay looked great but this place is stunning. You really could've been an interior designer for the rich and famous."

Lila's face reddened with Cara's compliment. "Thank you, for such a lovely compliment. After leaving the stresses of the office, it's wonderful to come home to my sanctuary."

"That you have my friend," making her way to the glass dining table where Lila had just placed their dinner, sinking into the thick oversized cushioned chairs. "The scent emanating from that large bouquet I passed in your living room is delightful. What are those?"

"English lavender. It's my new favourite flower. Let's eat while everything is still nice and hot."

Slicing through the mushroom gravy sauce into the thick piece of steak, Cara closed her eyes as the juicy meat made its way inside her mouth. Savouring the flavours as she chewed and swallowed, Cara looked at Lila "Girl, you've outdone yourself and I'm sure the asparagus wrapped in prosciutto is going to be just as spectacular. Asparagus is one of my favourite veggies, until I have to pee." Giggling together, Cara and Lila finished their meals with little chatter as both seemed lost within each delicious bite.

With the dishes cleaned away, they grabbed spots across from one another on the couches. Even though it had been a warm day for the middle of August, Lila's fuzzy throw blanket felt good over Cara's legs as she sipped on her tea in the air-conditioned room.

"So fill me in Lila, how's it been lately with your Dad?"

"It's been quite amazing having him back in my life. We've had to have some pretty deep conversations, but being open and vulnerable with one another, and sharing everything that both of us went through has only brought us closer. He's been really sweet and has even offered to take me to my last two follow-up appointments with Dr. Munro."

"I think that's wonderful, Lila and I couldn't be happier for you. You deserve the best, my friend."

"Thank you, Cara, but enough about me and my Dad, this get-together was to celebrate you."

"We certainly have a lot to be thankful for, Lila."

"That we do."

CHAPTER 20

Traveling Together

WIPING DOWN HER granite kitchen countertops Cara sang along to Pink pumping out from her Bluetooth speaker, feeling confident in her vocals since the kids were outside playing, leaving no one to hear her. Lifting the bowl of fruit off the island, she wiped away the little ring beneath it when the loud Bing through the speaker startled her. Pulling out her best dance moves over to her cell phone on the coffee table, she was surprised to see a text from Jay. It wasn't his weekend coming up with the kids, so she wondered why he was messaging. Lowering the volume, happy to take a little rest, she sat on the couch to read what he had sent.

Hey Cara, since the kids are on summer break, I would like to take them on a weeklong camping trip. Would the last week in August work with their schedules?

At the thought she might have an opportunity to spend an entire week with Angel, Cara wanted to do backflips around her living room even though she knew she could barely pull off a somersault at the best of times. Clicking on Angel's name in messages, she quickly fired her a text. *I just received the best news ever. Jay wants to take the kids camping for a week at the end of August. Is there any chance your kids might be able to spend that week with their dad too, so maybe you and I could plan a holiday together?* Cara turned the music high and started dancing around the room in anticipation of Angel's reply. It wasn't even twenty minutes when her Bing came through.

Book the flights, baby. We're going!

Jumping up and down, barely able to contain herself and almost dropping the phone, Cara texted Jay. *That last week works perfectly, Jay. The kids will love that.*

⁓≈⁓

As they boarded their flight, Angel looked over at Cara. "I can't believe we're doing this. We get to spend five whole days and nights together in San Diego!"

"I promised you we would go one day, Angel. It's going to be amazing."

They arrived to warm winds, palm tree-lined streets and the sun setting, casting an orange-yellow hue across the horizon. Cara had booked one of the fourteen cottages at the Blue Pier Inn.

"Look at the entrance sign, Angel. *Sleep over the Ocean*"

"This is going to be spectacular!"

"Each cottage is so private from the others, and look, we have an oceanfront view. Let's check out the inside, Angel."

"Oh my God, Cara, look at all the white shiplap on the walls. It makes this place look so quaint and beachy."

"Check out that white comforter in the bedroom."

Angel did, then fell backward onto the bed. "I've never been on one so thick. We are going to have some fun on this tonight."

Cara's attention was drawn to a picture on the bedroom wall of a beach chair nestled in the sand. Printed across the bottom was, *How beautiful it is to do nothing, and then rest afterward.* "I'm in love with this place Angel."

When they walked back into the living area, there was a beautiful bouquet and two bottles of Pinot Noir wine Cara hadn't noticed on the first go-round. The vase held soft blue, pink, and yellow carnations with three long-petal white daisies spread throughout. Cara's first thought was that this was part of the booking until she read the card: *Cara, cheers to the first of hopefully many adventures together. Love, Angel.*

Cara's heart was overfilled with emotion. The thought that Angel had taken the time to call in advance and set it up so that flowers, wine, and a special card were there upon their arrival was just the loveliest thing she thought anyone had ever done for her. She had never needed nor wanted grand gestures proving someone loved her. Simple actions like this made her feel loved and that she was worth the effort. She turned to Angel and held her hands. "From the bottom of my heart, thank you for arranging such a touching gesture. It is so thoughtful and feels so incredibly special that you organized it for me." Pulling Angel in close, Cara kissed her with as much passion as she could. "God, I love you."

"And I love you."

After a bottle of white wine and an evening of uninterrupted unforgettable moments, they drifted off to the sound of waves rhythmically crashing against the pier beams below.

With the morning sun's brightness bringing them out of their cozy slumber, they jumped up simultaneously and hurried outside to take in their ocean view. Leaning against the deck's horizontal white rails, Cara snuggled into Angel's back, inhaling the heavenly scent of last night's pleasures, while watching the early surfers catch their waves.

They spent the better part of the morning sitting together, Angel resting her back on Cara's chest, wrapped in a cream velour blanket on one of the blue-and-white cushioned deck loungers.

"I could stay with you forever like this, Cara! Being with you is the most beautiful thing I have ever experienced. I love the softness of your skin against my skin. Everything about being with you is sensual and sexy. I can't imagine ever being with a man again."

"Well, I'm thankful for that."

"Just thinking about it, Cara makes me want to gag! Their hairy bodies. All their spitting and farting and to never have to give a blowjob again! You have no idea how thankful I am that you're in my life."

"I feel the same way, Angel. I couldn't be happier that we have found each other!"

"Shall we go get some breakfast?"

"Yes, let's. I noticed a little restaurant just outside the gate of our place when we came in last night. Why don't we check that out?"

Sky's Café turned out to be a quaint restaurant with its menus written on surfboards hanging from the ceiling. After not being able to eat one more piece of bacon or slice of toast smothered in melted peanut butter, they decided to go for a long walk, hoping to find the famous Hotel del Coronado where classic movie stars like Cary Grant, Marilyn Monroe, and Katherine Hepburn used to stay back in the fifties. Every day they were tourists finding new spots to shop, eat, or grab a few drinks, and every night, they made love, the connection drawing Cara further in.

"When we fly back home this afternoon, Cara, I'll miss waking up to you each morning." A pout forming on her lips, Angel said, "After today, it's back to reality."

"Well, the reality isn't here just yet", pulling Angel in close, slowly lifting her tank top, smiling as her luscious, lip-smacking nipples dropped into view. Cara used her tongue and mouth to make Angel moan as she worked her way around her breasts and down her tight stomach. Pausing momentarily, she looked up at Angel, as she slid her thumbs under either side of her bikini panties, dropping them to the floor in one quick motion. Licking her lips and inhaling Angel's sweet scent, Cara dove in, providing Angel with one more holiday memory.

CHAPTER 21

Something's Changing

※

CARA FELT THE shift but didn't understand why it was happening. Nothing had felt the same since their return four months earlier from San Diego. Instead of their relationship gaining steam, it felt like Angel was pulling away.

Cara sat on her couch in the same clothes she had worn for the past three days. The kids would be home from school soon, but she didn't feel like getting up and making dinner. Looking around the room she saw that the past day's breakfast, lunch, and dinner dishes had surpassed the rim of the sink and were now spilling onto the counter. The smell of the garbage should've been reason enough to put her in motion, but neither that nor the dust on her furniture motivated her.

Ring…

"Hello."

"Hey, Cara."

Sitting up from her slouched position, "I'm so glad you called, Angel. How are you doing? It feels like forever since we've talked."

"I've had a crazy couple of weeks, and my migraines are back, so I haven't been feeling great."

"I'm so sorry to hear that. I wish you'd let me know when you aren't feeling good. I feel left out of your life when you don't share what's happening or allow me to be there for you."

"That's selfish of you, Cara! You should think less about yourself and more about me and how I'm feeling during those times."

"But that's what I'm trying to say. I truly care how you feel and want to be there for you when you've had a tough day at work or aren't feeling well. It feels like when those times are happening, you push me away instead of leaning on me for love and support."

"You're just overreacting, Cara. I don't have time for any more stress. I was calling to let you know I want this weekend for myself. I'm going to relax tomorrow night, and then on Saturday, I've decided to go with my sister to her friend's one-year-old daughter's birthday party."

"Really? You're going to go to a one-year-old birthday party instead of hanging out with me? I was so looking forward to spending this weekend with you."

"Plans change, Cara."

"Well, I'll be here if you change your mind or want to talk."

Cara hung up. *These are the times I need you, Mom. I've been waiting all week to see her, and what does she do, just like she's done so many times these last few months, she cancels on me last minute. She's choosing to go to a one-year-old's birthday party over spending time with me! I honestly feel like I'm becoming last on her priority list. I understand that plans aren't always going to work out, but this is getting ridiculous. We have only two weekends together each month when we don't have our kids. It's not like I'm asking to spend every minute of every day with her.*

Is it wrong that I'm feeling this way? Is Angel right and maybe I am overreacting? It feels like it's becoming a pattern with her because it starts the same way every time. First, her texts are less frequent, and if I try contacting her to see if anything's wrong, I get messages saying she's too busy, or it's not a good time to talk. She doesn't say when's a good time to text or call her, so I'm just left in the dark waiting for her to get in touch. If she's struggling, I want to support her, but she doesn't allow me to. She just makes me wait until she's ready to talk. That messes with my mind, Mom. What's even worse, is that lately when she does call me, it's usually to tell me she's cancelling our weekend again. You won't believe what she says to me when I remind her how important those weekends are to me: She'll actually tell me, "Your thoughts of how you think a relationship should be is a fairy tale way of thinking, Cara." Is my way of thinking foolish? Am I asking too much of her? All I feel lately is confused. I'm now finding it hard to even open up and share with her how certain things she does make me feel. No matter how I say it, she automatically goes into defensive mode and then attack mode, instead of just hearing what I'm trying to share with her. I get so frustrated with myself because I allow her reactive words toward me to affect how I communicate my thoughts to her. I get all flustered, and I jumble my words. Ultimately, she has a way of making me feel wrong for even bringing my concerns up. Am I being selfish, Mom, for letting her know how I feel?

Cara's phone pinged with a text from Angel: *So tired of hearing the disappointment in your voice. I can't seem to do anything right, and I will not apologize for it. I made a commitment to myself at the beginning of this year, that I will only do things that feel right to me. No more guilt or feeling torn, whether it's from kids, my mom, my sister, or you. The weekends I don't have the kids still belong to me, and I will make choices on what I do, based on how I feel.*

Cara's mouth dropped open. But there was more: *I'm not living another day feeling like I've done something wrong when I haven't. I love being with you and having you by my side, but I won't allow myself to change into someone I'm not or feel bad for the choices I make to be with someone. Life is just too short.*

Cara was flabbergasted. She texted Angel back: *Angel, hearing you say the weekends that I don't have the kids still belong to me, and I will make choices on what I do based on how it makes me feel, makes me think you and I are not on the same page when it comes to what was supposed to be our time. I have always looked at the weekends I don't have my kids not as time that belongs to me, because I have twenty-six other days in the month for myself, my kids, my friends, and anything else I need to do. The weekends I don't have the kids have always been about spending as much of that time as possible with you. I always check to see if it is our weekend before I plan anything. If it is our weekend and an event comes up, I talk with you first before any decision is made. Those weekends, we agreed, would be our time to help build our relationship because we don't have the luxury of seeing each other whenever we want. When you decide on your own that you will do whatever you want without making me part of the decision, that hurts me and makes me feel insecure about us. It makes me feel that I am not a priority in your life. I am not trying to make you feel bad and I have no issues whatsoever with you spending time with your family and friends. I just wish you would choose any other day to be with them than on one of the four days we get to spend quality time together. For all the time I don't get to see you, I wish the time set aside for us was as important to you as it is to me. You have been very honest with me in your text, and I respect that, and that is why I am being honest with you and sharing how I feel.*

No reply came back from Angel.

Having felt lost all weekend, Cara's spirits were slightly elevated from Lila's and Sophie's immediate replies that they would be happy to meet her this afternoon for coffee at Cafe Beano. Sunday proved to be another cold one. Waiting inside at a table for four in the back, Cara sat anxiously, drowning in her thoughts as she warmed her hands on a steaming cup of hot chocolate. Seeing Lila and Sophie come through the door shaking snow from their toques and jackets as they made their way toward her, Cara forced a smile. She'd invited Angel but since Angel was in no contact mode again, she had no idea if she would be joining them this afternoon.

"Hey, Lila! Hey Sophie. Thanks for meeting with me so last minute."

"Well, I had plans to please myself with an orgasm this afternoon, but I thought for you guys, it could wait."

Lila shook her head. "So glad our coffee date was more important, Sophie."

"Will Angel be joining us?" Sophie asked.

"I'm not sure," Cara said.

"Shit, Cara, the only way you know that girl is going to attend anything is when you see her driving up!"

With lips pressed together, Cara looked up to the ceiling, and moved her head up and down, letting out a big sigh. "I need to ask you guys something."

Lila put her hand on Cara's shoulder. "What's up, Cara? You look sad."

Cara needed to figure out a way to share what had been going on between her and Angel without them knowing it was a lover's spat. "It's Angel, for a while now, she hasn't been treating me all that well. This past weekend she cancelled our plans again, and when I shared with her how that made me feel, she told me I was overreacting and being selfish."

"What the fuck, Cara!" Sophie said. "You are by far the least selfish person I know. You're always there for us when we need you."

"Sophie's right, Cara. You don't deserve to be talked to or treated like that. I think you should reach out to Angel and talk all this through."

"I've tried, Lila, but she doesn't respond."

"Let's hope it's just a one-off."

"I wish that were the case, Lila, but this has been happening a lot lately. I know she will return to her old self again, but it plays with my mind when she does this to me. I start thinking maybe it *is* me, and I am overreacting."

"It's not you, Cara, and Angel needs to stop treating you like that," Lila said, reaching in and giving Cara a big hug.

"Thanks guys, I so appreciate both of you. I hope things do change because I like Angel and I don't want to lose her from my life."

CHAPTER 22

Angel

S‍ITTING IN THE parking lot of the kid's school, Cara was mad at herself for allowing her emotions to get the better of her. Dani had taken a little longer that morning getting ready for school trying to decide what she should wear for a crazy dress-up day. Instead of Cara helping and being excited with her about the fun day ahead, Cara was more concerned that they were going to be late and kept on Dani to hurry up. Once they were in the vehicle and on their way, Cara felt the need to give Dani a lecture about being more responsible, prepared and organized which only infuriated Dani because she didn't think it was that big of a deal. When they arrived at school and were only five minutes late, Cara wanted to kick herself for making a mountain out of a molehill. She had been short with the kids all weekend which was so out of character for her, but because another weekend had gone by and she still hadn't heard from Angel, she had been in a funky mood. Cara picked up her cell phone and punched in Angel's number.

"Ya, what's up?"

"Hey, Angel, I haven't heard from you for over a week. I just wanted to check in to make sure you're doing okay."

"I'm fine, Cara. You know I have a life outside of you, right."

"I know you do, Angel, but I was a little concerned because normally, you would have texted me by now."

"You're becoming very needy, Cara. I have lots of important things going on. I can't just drop everything because you need a text from me. My week has been busy with the kids and work is always steady. I don't have as much free time as you."

"I've been missing you, Angel, and it's been well over a week since we've seen each other."

"It's not that big of a deal, Cara. Look, I can't deal with this right now. I'll text you when I'm not so busy."

Doesn't Cara understand that her needs aren't important to me? The only needs of any interest to me are my own. If she wants to be with me, she needs to be more concerned about what I want and less about what she wants. She might be missing me, but I'm completely fine not seeing her. If I'm being honest, the only thing I've missed lately is some playtime with her and I know exactly what to say to get some of that.

Bing: Angel's name popped up on Cara's cell as she was trying to focus on getting some business work off her desk. Her attempts to complete the work on Monday, Tuesday, Wednesday, and Thursday had failed because her motivation level was nonexistent, but today she was determined to face the pile head-on and get it done. Cara stopped what she was doing to look at Angel's text.

Hey, Cara, I hope the week has gone well for you. I'd like to spend some time with you tonight and was hoping you could meet me at OJ's for a drink at seven.

Cara read the message a second time. *Am I going crazy? Did Angel not just ignore me for days and now she's texting me like nothing happened? No explanation, no apology for keeping me in the dark all week. Nothing but a text asking me out. I'm upset with her, but I've also really missed her and I know from experience if I bring anything up she'll renege on the invite, so I guess I'll meet up with her.*

That evening, Angel was standing just outside the front doors of OJ's, as Cara pulled up in her car. Tentatively walking toward Angel, she saw a big smile on her face, which instantly caused Cara's shoulders to drop and her pace to pick up.

"Hi, Cara, it's so good to see you." Angel hugged her, holding on just a little longer than Cara. Oh, how Cara loved it when she did that. It made her feel like Angel never wanted to let her go. She immediately was in a better frame of mind from that hug.

They found a raised table for two in the far corner. Once their drink order had been placed, Angel spoke first.

"I want to clarify and be clear about what I meant in my text the other week. Please know, Cara, I want to be in a relationship with you, so you don't need to feel insecure about us. I'm going to try harder to stop making you feel that way because all I ever picture is the two of us together. From now on, let's stop texting when important issues arise and instead, let's always talk to each other in person. If we do that, there will be less confusion in the meaning behind our words."

"I couldn't agree with you more, Angel and I want you to know that I, too, am fully vested in our relationship and when future issues arise, I want to talk through them with you when they happen and do whatever it takes to make our relationship work."

"I'm glad we are on the same page, Cara. Let's finish these drinks and head to my place. Both kids won't be back from their friends until around 11…wanna?"

"Cheque!"

CHAPTER 23

Everything Feels Back on Track

CARA FELT SO refreshed after another great sleep. It was only 11 a.m. but she was already caught up on all the day's paperwork. Having had breakfast early that morning, her belly was letting her know loudly that lunch was needed soon.

Thoughts of Angel drifted through her mind. These last few weeks had Cara feeling their relationship was back on track. Angel was following through on her words, providing Cara with the reassurance she needed to feel safe and secure in their relationship. *It would be nice to see Angel today. I'm going to see if she can join me for lunch.*

Ring…

"Hello?"

"Hey Angel, do you have time from work today to meet at your place for lunch? I could make us a nice salad."

"You bet; I can be there around 12:15."

"Sounds great! See you then."

When Angel walked in the door, Cara was there to greet her with a huge hug and a big fat kiss.

"How's the day been for you?" Cara asked.

"It's been pretty busy; this is such a nice break."

Both Cara and Angel shared stories of their mornings and when Cara finished talking about something that had happened with Cody, Angel jumped in.

"I wanted to share with you that I've been stressing a bit about my mom's memory lately. It seems to be getting worse."

"I'm sure that feels a little scary for you, Angel. You know I've been through all those moments with my mom, so when you're not sure how to handle something, let me know and I'll do my best to give you some tips. We got this!"

"I'm just worried that with everything happening to my mom, it's going to affect our time together?"

In that instant, all Cara heard was, *I'm not going to have time for us; all my extra time will have to go to my mom.* That thought filled Cara's eyes with tears.

"Oh my gosh, Cara, I'm so sorry for making you sad. Come over here; let me hug you."

Cara held on to Angel tightly, thinking if she let go, she would lose her. She wanted to share with Angel what she was feeling at that moment, but she knew if she tried, she would not be able to hold back the tears, and she couldn't let that happen.

I'm sorry to leave you like this, Cara, but forty-five minutes has just flown by and I need to head back to work now…let me give you one more big hug."

"Thanks for the hug, Angel. I'll tidy up our lunch stuff before I leave."

Before closing the door, Angel looked back at Cara and said, "I love you. Cara."

"Love you too."

Wiping down the counter, Cara's mind was spinning. *Why did my emotions kick in like that, Mom? Why did I go directly to the thought that Angel won't have time for me? She didn't say that, yet I automatically went there. Why am I so afraid of losing her?*

After putting everything away and pulling herself back into a better head space, Cara headed for home.

At 5:15 that evening, Cara's phone rang.

"Hello."

"I think that was very selfish of you, Cara, putting yourself first today when I was telling you something that was affecting me with my mom."

Cara had been beating herself up mentally all afternoon for how she'd handled herself. Her emotions had taken her by surprise. "I'm so sorry for the way I acted…please forgive me."

"All I wished was when I got home today, you would have left a note saying everything is going to be okay."

"Angel, I shouldn't have reacted how I did, and again I am so sorry. My emotions came on so fast, and for some reason, I felt overwhelmed by the thought of you not having time for me anymore. I wanted to tell you what I felt, but I couldn't express it because I was fighting back my tears. Please, please forgive me."

"I need you to hear me when I share something with you, Cara, and don't just think about yourself."

"Again, I'm sorry, Angel."

To make up for how she had acted, Cara went out the next day and bought Angel a beautiful fishbowl vase filled with pink and red roses. She brought it to Angel's house and left it on her nightstand along with a little note: *I hear you, Angel, and I'm very sorry for how I acted yesterday. I am here for you and will always be by your side to support you when you need it. Love you always.* Cara hoped it would be a happy surprise for Angel when she returned from work that day.

CHAPTER 24

Blindsided

FRIDAY MORNING, CARA woke to see a message from Angel on her phone: *Hi, Cara ☺ This weekend, I'm going to hang out alone—I feel like I need some time for myself. I hope you understand.*

Cara wanted to respect what Angel had shared earlier that week about hearing her when she said she needed something. *Absolutely! I hope the weekend gives you exactly what you need. Call if you feel like talking, and I hope you have a great weekend.* Cara understood that Angel needed time for herself, and a quiet weekend would give her that.

On Monday morning, Cara woke to a text from Angel saying, *Hi, I hope you had a great weekend. How is your morning so far?*

Hi ☺ So far, so good. How are you feeling?

Head sucks! This weather is seriously killing me. I just want to crawl under my blankets. ☹ Hopefully, the medication will kick in soon.

I hope your head clears up quickly for you.

That night, Cara texted, *Goodnight, Angel*, but received no reply.

The following day, Cara received a *Morning Cara* ☺ text.

Morning Angel ☺ *I'm off to Brooks to check on some of my properties.*

I'm in Claresholm today for some meetings.

I didn't think you had to go out of town this week for work.

Me either; it's nice, though, to be away from the office ☺ *Although I have to go back today and get organized for the job fair on Wednesday. How's your day?*

My day has been great…thanks for asking. Is it busy in the Claresholm office?

My client is late or not coming, so it's great! I'm just passing the time until I head back. Good day so far.

That's great!

Later that afternoon, as Cara was driving down the main street in Okotoks, she spotted Angel driving by in the opposite direction. When she was stopped at the next red light, she quickly sent her a text: *Just passed you…on my way to Dani's basketball tournament.*

A reply came back instantly: *Didn't see you.*

Dani's team ended up winning the gold medal game at the tournament, and Cara was excited to share the great news with Angel, so she sent off a text, *Dani won gold!!!!*

Angel replied, *Awesome!*

That evening at around 8:20, Cara texted Angel: *How's the head feeling tonight?*

It's okay. How are you?

Cara was tired of texting and wanted to hear Angel's voice, so she texted: *Can you talk?*

Angel's reply was long: *Cara, I want you to know I have tried hard to be what you need. I want you to find what you need and to be happy. It's hard to let go when I love you so much, but we always end up back at this point. Just let this happen and see what new adventure awaits you. I will always be here for you. I hope you will be my forever and always friend xo.*

The reply hit Cara like a brick across the face. WTF! Where in the world was this coming from? After all their recent conversations about being together and wanting to do whatever it took, Angel was arbitrarily deciding she didn't want to be with her anymore and thought it was okay to tell her in a text. A text was something a sixth grader would do to someone they had been dating for a couple of weeks and to finish the text with, *I hope you will be my forever and always friend…*WTF!

Cara's mind was in turmoil. She thought: *What the mother fucking fuck!!!! Why hadn't Angel just picked up the phone or met to talk if something had been bothering her? Why did she continue to text back and forth, even using fucking smiley faces in her messages, only to dump my ass in a fucking text? Was it all lies the other week when she told me all she ever pictured was the two of us together? Hell, Angel said we needed to talk in person if we had any issues in the future. What fucked-up game is she playing? What kind of person does this to their partner? I gave her exactly what she asked for this past weekend and still, it wasn't enough. Angel doesn't do things to benefit us as a couple; Angel does what is best for Angel, with no fucking consideration for anyone else but herself.*

Cara's blood was boiling. If Angel didn't want her anymore, fuck her!

Her anger amplified as she walked throughout her home, seeing pictures of them together and little mementos of places and things they had shared. Cara grabbed every memory, piece by piece, threw them all in a bag and tossed them in her closet. The thought that Angel didn't want her anymore and that she was so easily disposable that it could be done in a text made Cara question if she had ever meant anything to Angel.

It only took a day for Cara's emotions to swing in the opposite direction. She was on her way home from dropping Dani and Cody off at their friends' houses when out of nowhere, deep-rooted sadness clenched her entire being, and like a shaken can of Coke, Cara's tears exploded. The fear of having no one felt like falling from the ledge of a cliff with no parachute to break the fall. Her self-created mind box, constructed from childhood and used throughout her life to bury any perceived emotional pain so she wouldn't have to feel it, was not working for her this time. As Cara's car passed each broken white paint strip on the roadway back to her house, the box she created started to crumble, causing her to lose all control of her emotions.

Pulling into her gravel driveway, she ran, shaking, from her vehicle, collapsing on her bed in a fetal position. A tsunami of emotions crashed down on her with an intensity Cara had never felt. The loss of her innocence, the loss of her marriage, the loss of her mom, and now the loss of Angel. Tortured sounds escaped Cara's lips. Sounds she had never before made. At that moment, she understood 'broken-hearted' because her heart physically hurt within her chest from the thoughts she was experiencing: *Angel doesn't love me. She doesn't want me and now I'm going to be alone. I thought she was my person. I thought we were going to grow old together! What am I supposed to do now? What can I do to make Angel understand how much she means to me? I need to talk to her. I need to let her know how much I love her and want her in my life. Do I call her? Should I text her? Maybe I should go see her personally? I want to do it right, but what is the right way for Angel? I'll call her; that's what I'll do. She said we should talk personally if it's something important.*

She called and got Angela's voicemail. *Doesn't matter, I'm still going to let her know how I feel.*

Beep… "My heart hurts, Angel. The future was supposed to be you and me together. This is killing me! You are what I need, and you truly make me happy. Ending back at the same point means there are things we haven't quite worked out yet. There will always be issues throughout our lives that we'll need to work on because that is how relationships grow. You work through rough times to strengthen your relationship when you love someone. I know that together you and I can get through anything. I don't want to just 'let this happen' and see what new adventures await me. All my experiences have been with you. All the fantastic memories have been made with you. My future is being a partner with you. I told you I was all in on our relationship, and that won't change. Others in your life may not have fought for you, but that's not me. I want you in my life, and I am willing to do whatever it takes to keep us together. I love you, Angel. Please don't give up on us. Call or meet with me so we can talk."

Two days passed with no response from Angel.

Cara couldn't sleep or eat, and her hair looked greasy as she paced past the hall mirror for the hundredth time. *Why hadn't she been a better partner for Angel? If only she could talk face-to-face with her, that would help change Angel's mind. It can't end this way.*

Cara showered, practicing what she would say as the water beat on the top of her head.

She drove to Angel's house. She stood at Angel's front door and knocked tentatively, relaxing ever so slightly when the door opened, and she saw a smile break across Angel's face.

Did she see a smile or was that a smirk?

Angel invited her in, providing Cara with the slightest hope that she was open to having a conversation with her.

"Can I please give you a hug, Angel?"

She was receptive, so Cara took the moment and held on, thinking it might be the last hug she ever got to give Angel. Cara could feel her heart bouncing off Angel's chest as she held her in the foyer.

They sat down at the kitchen table. Cara didn't have a chance to speak as Angel immediately jumped in: "Cara, it still feels like you aren't listening to me. I came home from work last week to see Cody sitting on my couch watching TV."

Cara had to take a minute to process what Angel was talking about. Cara remembered dropping Cody off at Angel's house after school the week before because she had some running around in town and didn't want Cody to sit in the car and wait for her. She had called Angel's daughter, Jayden who was home that day, to ask if it was okay that Cody hung out upstairs until she was finished with her errands. After getting her okay, she texted Angel to give her the heads up that Cody would be there for a bit and that she would pick him up as soon as she was done running around. Angel hadn't texted back, so Cara hadn't given it another thought.

"I would have preferred if you'd asked me instead of just assuming I would be okay with it. I have been struggling with migraines, and I wasn't happy to come home to see Cody on my couch, watching TV and eating some chips he'd gotten from my cupboard."

Cara couldn't believe this was something Angel was bringing up for why she didn't want to be in a partnership with her anymore. Cara had always done so much for Angel. She drove Jayden home almost every other day from school, even buying her and her sister dinner sometimes when she knew Angel would be late at work. Cara couldn't remember a time she hadn't been there for Angel, and here Angel was upset at Cara for not asking her for permission…even though Cara had sent her a text.

"I also can't believe you didn't text me yesterday to ask how my job fair went at work."

Cara sat stunned. Angel's job fair had occurred after Angel had dumped her, yet Angel still expected Cara to text her asking how the job fair went. *That comment of Angels sounded borderline insane, Did she actually think it was normal to one day be in a committed partnership to then, the next day be buddies asking each other how their day went. Had their relationship meant absolutely nothing to her.* Cara just sat there and listened as Angel went on.

"I felt good not sharing last weekend with you. It felt good to hang out with my sister and not worry about how you would feel. I could do whatever I wanted. You would've been upset because that would have taken up our weekend time. You would've been happy to see my sister, but you would've been excited for her to leave too so you could have that time with just me."

"You're right, Angel. I've told you how important to me that time together is."

Angel didn't miss a beat. "All the other days I'm not with you, I have my kids, so when I don't have them, I want to be able to do things with my mom or my sister. I want to be able to go for a drink with them because I'm not able to drink around my kids and feel relaxed."

As Cara sat there, she was brought back to a conversation with Angel when they'd first started dating. She remembered telling Angel how important it was to have friends and a life outside their relationship because that was healthy. Cara had no issue with Angel spending time with her family or her one friend. What she couldn't understand was why Angel could not find time to do all those things she was telling Cara she wanted to do, during the time the two of them weren't together. Angel's kids were old enough to be on their own for a few hours at home if she wanted to go out. Angel was making it look like Cara was preventing her from doing what she wanted, which was both unfair and untrue. Angel was not being honest with herself by acknowledging the real issue, which was she tended to drink more than she should, and that was why she didn't feel relaxed going out drinking if her kids were home. Angel had shared with Cara in the past that Jayden, would frequently tell her that she drank too much and instead of Angel taking responsibility for her actions and figuring out a way to change what she was doing, it was easier to make Cara the scapegoat for her issues.

"I feel pressured by you, Cara, to be with you, which is now making me not want to be with you."

"How does asking for four days out of an entire month put pressure on you, Angel? I love spending any time I get with you. I make myself available whenever you want to spend time with me and all I wish is that you felt the same."

"I feel numb about us right now, Cara and I'm okay with not being together."

Angel's damaging words, felt like a knife stabbed deep into Cara's gut. Still wanting to try and salvage what she thought they'd once had, Cara knew Angel well enough to suck it up and accept responsibility for how Angel felt. She knew if she tried to justify, explain, or clarify any further, it would accomplish nothing and only anger Angel more.

Cara looked at Angel. "Because we've kept us, a secret and not told our kids, that has hurt our relationship. We should let our kids know, and that way, we can be open to seeing each other whenever. Then you won't have to feel pressured about those four days."

"I will not be telling them. I brought a man into my son's life when he was only three, and I have always regretted doing that. I will not make the same mistake with the two girls. Even if I were with a man now, I wouldn't bring him into their lives."

Angel's so-called logic made zero sense to Cara. Angel had already told her sister, her mom, and her son, about their relationship and they were all fine. Her daughters were old enough to understand. "I believe if we talk to our kids, we could have a chance at a normal relationship. Everything about *us* is clouded under secrecy because we are not out, and that causes a lot of added pressure." Cara knew if she didn't say the right things now, she would lose Angel forever. "Look, Angel, if you need to be with your mom or whomever during our weekends, that is something you need, and I will have to be okay with it. I will also try my best to listen to your needs, and I will try not to cause you any extra pressure."

"How is this time different? Why do you think you will be okay with not seeing me as much this time?"

Cara breathed in deeply. "You know how I compartmentalize things, so I don't allow my feelings to get the best of me."

"Yes."

"Well, when I thought about not having you in my life, I cried hysterically for the first time. Even when my mom died, I didn't allow myself to grieve that loss and instead pushed that pain down deep inside before it had a chance to rain on me, all because I didn't want to feel that pain. When my marriage fell apart, I did not grieve that loss either and instead put on a brave face and did whatever I needed to do to move forward. From a young age, I learned to shut down my emotions to stay strong, but that was not the case the other day when I thought about losing you. I couldn't push that thought into the box. Losing you felt so immense to me that I physically and mentally broke down." Cara had never been so vulnerable or transparent about her past or her feelings, but none of what she'd said fazed Angel. Angel just looked right through her with the dullest, dead dark-brown eyes and said, "I'm good with my decision."

I'm so thankful I don't have to think of anyone but myself right now. Listening to Cara go on and on about how she broke down because she couldn't bear to be without me…of course, she can't bear it; it would be hard to live without me. I don't even care if she's hurting. It doesn't affect me in the least. Hopefully, she finally understands that I will never truly love her. I always acted like I did to make sure my needs were fulfilled, but love her, that was never going to happen.

CHAPTER 25

Online Dating

Cara knew the relationship was over, but in her heart, she was still figuring out how to move forward. It had been months since their breakup, yet still in her quiet moments, the almost-closed door had a way of swinging back open. She would relive the beautiful times the two of them had shared, causing her to second-guess what had led to the demise of their relationship. Could she have done something differently or handled situations better? Should she have fought harder to win Angel's love and attention? The would-haves, could-haves and should-haves, ate away at Cara in those moments, causing her to beat herself up with the feeling that if she had done things differently, she wouldn't be sitting all alone and instead would still have Angel by her side. The hardest part for Cara was that she had no one to share these thoughts with. Her relationship with Angel had been a secret to everyone in her life, so the struggle had to be handled on her own.

I'm done with these thoughts, it's almost the end of June and I need to do something to start moving forward. Everyone else seems to be doing it, I might as well too! Popping onto her computer, Cara brought up Match.com and started filling in her details. When it came to choosing *Interested in men or women*, Cara paused. Even though she was still attracted to men, the idea of being with one intimately was no longer appealing to her. Choosing 'women' and then filling in the rest of the required answers to the long list of questions, Cara finally hit the complete button. Automatically up popped pictures of all the available women. Scrolling past a barrage of them that held zero attraction to Cara, she stopped when she came across a photo of a pretty lady named Natasha. Figuring it was now or never, Cara composed her first message:

Hi, Natasha, my name is Cara, and this is my first time trying online dating. Lucky or not, LOL, you are the first person I am emailing. I saw your picture and was intrigued, but your bio made me want to subscribe to the site so I might have the opportunity to meet you. I am also an amazing, well-adjusted woman who would like to meet someone special to build a relationship with. I LOVE the sun, staying fit, and having fun! I can be goofy but also responsible and professional when needed. Your write-up made me laugh, which is one of life's most important things. If you're happy, life is great! I, too, am bad at remembering names and don't care for waiting in lines, but I am a pretty good singer, especially when alone in my car ;) I think we have a fair bit in common, and if you are interested, I would like to get together for a walk to talk.

Thirty minutes later the reply came: *Hi, Cara, Thanks for your message. Glad I was able to make you laugh. A day without laughter is a day wasted, or so I think! If you don't mind chatting a bit, to get to know each other first, I feel more comfortable that way. Your profile mentions you are still separated, and it sounds like from a man. Have you been in a relationship with a woman before? Pardon my bluntness. Many curious women have approached me, and that's not what I'm into—just looking for some clarity. Yes, being happy is so important; life is too short. So being able to relax and enjoy the moment or be the goofball if the moment allows…why not? I used to think I was a good singer until I got a dog. She gives me a look and walks away! Chat soon!*

Cara was excited to reply. *Hi, Natasha, thanks for taking the time to reply to my message. Chatting first is the perfect way to get to know each other better. I appreciate you getting right to the point and asking me about being with a man and if I have been in a relationship with a woman. You, like me, know what we want at this stage in life, so why waste time? Yes, I married a man and we had two beautiful children together. After many years of marriage, my feelings toward him changed. I was the one who wanted out, so I left. If you decide you would like to keep chatting with me, I am willing to share more about that part of my life. If I have been in a relationship with a woman, yes, I have. Once that Pandora's box was opened, I was all in! I am not curious, and I am not a one-night-stand kind of gal. If a person is important to me as a friend or in a relationship, I put everything into it. What I need, though, is to know and feel through words and actions that the other person wants to put in the same effort to make me feel wanted and loved too. I hope this clarifies a little bit about myself. If you would like to share some of your stories with me, I would like to hear them. On a side note, don't feel bad about the look your dog gave you…she might've had a bit of gas! Hope to hear from you.*

Natasha soon wrote back. *Hi, Cara. My Pandora's box was opened a long time ago! I was in my early twenties when I figured things out. Told my family a few years later. Growing up in a small Catholic French community, and being very close with my family, made it very scary to be me. But I strongly believe a healthy life is a true, honest, and genuine one…so, I told them, fully expecting rejection. To my surprise, all went well. My entire family is very supportive and welcoming of any partner I've had. I'm comfortable and never ashamed of who I am, but I don't announce it to the world every time I step out my front door. I often forget I am not like the norm. Maxine (my dog) thinks I'm perfect! ;) Everyone in my life, personal and colleagues, knows. I don't announce it to my clients, yet if they were to ask, I would be honest. There is nothing more confusing and hurtful to me than hearing the words "I love you" yet never feeling them from the other person. Actions do speak louder than words! It's important to know what you need in a relationship; it sounds like you do. I believe all five of the love languages are important for a balanced/healthy relationship. That said, my top two are quality time and physical touch. I've been told by past partners, friends, and colleagues that I am an excellent communicator. Although I'm sure, there is room for improvement! ;) I find it challenging to bond with someone if they put up walls. I've broken too many walls down in my past trying to get to the person's core. It's essential to me that my partner can communicate. Do your children know? I would imagine that's a bit challenging to sort out. Does your ex know? Is it amicable? Are you originally from Calgary? Have family here? Tell me a bit about your likes. It sounds like we both like the sun, so we are both lizards in a past life! Like to travel? Beach destinations? What do you like to do to stay fit? What activities do your children like?*

The first week of July had started out hot and Cara was enjoying the beautiful blue clear skies while walking along the country dirt roads near her home. Even though she was wearing shorts and a tank top, it still wasn't enough to keep her cool. Beads of sweat were dripping from her temples making her thankful she had brought her favourite soft pink plastic go-mug, filled with ice cold water.

Wanting to reply to Natasha's latest message, she pulled her phone out: *Hello, Natasha. It sounds like you have an amazing family. You are fortunate! Both my parents have passed. I loved them both, but I was extremely close to my mom, and I still miss her all the time. We had an amazing bond, both as mother/daughter and as friends ☺ I was still married when my parents passed, so they never knew. I, too, was raised in a Catholic household in a small town. My gut tells me they both would have been very accepting. When I look back on my life, there weren't any signs that made me think I would ever be involved with women, but that changed with time. I have never told my ex due to never wanting to hurt him, but I think he knows. We have an amicable relationship for our kids and business, but the relationship part of my life with him is over. I have kept this part of my life to myself. My kids don't know. They are getting older, and I have such a good relationship with them that I struggle to keep it from them. I know it will happen; I just need to find the right time. You mentioned that your top two love languages are quality time and physical touch. Those are mine too. I think to build a relationship, you need to spend time together. Time learning both the good and bad about each other. I know there probably isn't a lot bad about you because Maxine thinks you're perfect. I hope that what I have been saying shows I'm a pretty good communicator. I'm not perfect by any means, and I shut down when hurt. I don't like to answer things on the fly, but being given time to think about a situation allows me to gather my thoughts. I am always open to discussing anything if it helps keep the relationship strong. I love the sun, and my favourite place to travel is Costa Rica…but I would go anywhere hot! I go to the gym two to three times per week, and I try to get out hiking once a week (something new I picked up and enjoy). My daughter is a basketball player, and my son plays lacrosse…thanks for asking about them.* ☺

Natasha replied. Hi, Cara. Sorry to hear about your folks. Loss is a terrible thing. I admire those who can keep amicable with past partners. I would imagine it can't be easy at times. Yes, I can see how it is a struggle to tell your children—all in good time. ☺ *Oh, I am far from perfect and have a good list of my faults. But let's not tell Maxine and burst her bubble! ;) I agree; it's much harder to communicate when hurt or vulnerable. I've not been to Costa Rica yet. I quite like Mexico, fell in love with San Diego a few years back. So many beach destinations I've yet to visit. I must make my way to Hawaii soon! Oh, good for you! I've not been hiking in many years for several reasons that all sound like excuses! I need to get out there!* ☺ *What's* been your favourite hike so far? Both are fun sports for your kids! Do you or your kids follow their respective sports professionally? It sounds like you are an entrepreneur. I am looking forward to hearing more about that. Well, it's been a long day of work for me, and my brain is tired; I need rest. Chat soon.*

Cara replied the next morning. *Good morning, Natasha. I just wanted to thank you. Even though you were tired yesterday from work, you still took some time to answer my message. Those are the small, thoughtful things I so appreciate ☺ I will answer your questions in another message…just wanted to share something nice with you to start your day. I like the person you are showing me, and I am interested in finding out more about you.* ☺

Natasha's reply came quickly. *Hi, Cara, that was a very nice message; thank you! The feeling is mutual. My apologies but today has turned into quite a day already, and I am unexpectedly very busy with work. I want you to know I am enjoying getting to know you, and I wish you a wonderful day!* ☺ *Chat soon.*

Cara answered Natasha's questions in another message the following day. *Hi, Natasha. I hope you got through yesterday! You mentioned that you love San Diego…I've been there and stayed on the pier that has the little blue and white cottages on them. It's a fantastic place, and the area around it was so much fun! The weather in San Diego is beautiful. I like Mexico too, and I think Manzanillo and Mazatlán are my favourites. My first hot holiday ever was in Hawaii…it got me hooked on travelling to hot places. I'm sure you would love it. I always go with a friend who does all the guiding when I hike, so I don't remember the actual names of the ones I've been on, but the last one I was on was near Canmore and it was breathtaking at the top. A peanut butter sandwich never tastes so good as when you are at the top of a mountain looking at all that beauty! Both my kids like to watch the Calgary Roughnecks lacrosse. We have season tickets, so it is a fun night out for the three of us. Neither watches professional basketball on TV, but they like watching a professional football or basketball game live when the opportunity presents itself and so do*

I. Do you like sports? My business deals with rental properties. I purchase, renovate, and rent out long-term residential rentals. I did a few projects in the last couple of years that I was very involved in and loved doing, but due to the economy now, I don't have the funds to start anything new. If you'd like to share your work with me, I would be happy to hear about it. Here are a few things you don't know about me: I don't have any tattoos…I've thought about getting a small one, but it probably won't ever happen because I'm not into pain. I have a keen sense of smell, so I don't care to be around stinky people…I prefer as little amount of hair on a woman's body as possible…minus her head…hair there is good, lol. I love to kiss and cuddle. What excites me the most about a woman is her soft skin and soft kisses. I hope you are okay with me sharing the above… and I look forward to chatting with you soon when you have time.

Natasha replied late. *Good evening! Again, I'm mentally exhausted; I got home shortly after nine p.m. from work. My apologies for the delayed response. I'm a realtor. The brokerage I work for is very different from others. So much to type; we can get into details hopefully when we meet. I love real estate! I've been a realtor for ten years. San Diego is fun! I was recently in Mexico with my family. We rented a house in Playacar, which is right beside Playa del Carmen. It was paradise! I've never been to the other side of Mexico. I do like sports. I enjoy watching NFL, NBA, college basketball, and other sports. I love going to live games; the atmosphere is fun! I've been to one NFL game, one NBA game, and a few MLB games. I was fortunate to attend the March Madness Final for Men's NCAA basketball weekend. It was in Dallas, certainly a bucket list item for me! I occasionally go to Flames games and have been to a Roughnecks game. Those are fun! I do not have any tattoos and never plan on getting one. Like you, I'm not a fan of pain. Also, I don't find them appealing. Ha-ha, yes, stinky people are bad! I, too, have a strong sense of smell. I'm attracted to women who smell good! ☺ Agreed. No hair is good and much preferred! The smoother, the better. For myself and my partner. Kissing and cuddling are mandatory! Since I'm alone, Maxine puts up with a million kisses* on her forehead daily and I force her to snuggle when I can. Let's keep that our little secret, shall we? ;) Things you don't know about me: My favourite drink, other than something slushy, is red wine. I'm not a big drinker; I can't remember the last time I was tipsy. Probably a few years ago. I like to be the little spoon. I read every night before bed. I do not have a TV in the bedroom and hope never to have one there. Back to kissing…a good kisser is essential. I think intimate time should be romantic, sensual, and fun! I believe we have a lot in common…I best get to bed because I have another long day tomorrow. PS: I smile when I see a message from you.

Cara replied the next morning. *Good morning, Natasha* ☺ *It sounds like family is a big part of your life, and that's a good thing. I'm raising my kids to always be there for each other, and I am proud to say they have a fantastic friendship. I'm close to some of my brothers, but of course, with families, it's never perfect, so two of them I don't have any contact with. I don't have any extended family here…my brothers are spread all over Canada, and one even lives in England. It's nice to see that we do have a fair bit in common* ☺

Here are a few more things about me:

- *I am a tidy person…I like my house in order with beds made, and things picked up…a bit anal I know.*
- *I don't snore, but I like to sleep with a pillow between my legs.*
- *I like my back rubbed but only under my top, not on top of the shirt.*
- *My favourite alcoholic beverage is Bacardi white rum and Coke…next, I would choose a vodka club soda with a splash of cranberry (when watching calories). I enjoy having two or three drinks, but not regularly, and it is never a must-have. I am a happy social drinker!*
- *I'm sorry to say I do have a TV in my bedroom because that's what I prefer to do before falling asleep. Now, if I had*

someone there with me some evenings, watching TV would be far from my mind...
- *Being a good kisser...time will tell ;)*

I'm glad I bring a smile to your face when you see I have messaged you...that makes me happy. Have a great day, Natasha!

Natasha replied: *Yes, my family is very important to me. It's just my brother and me, but mom's side is big, so I have a lot of relatives. Close to most of them. That is so great to hear your kids have a good relationship. I'm not anal about cleanliness, but I keep a tidy home. Having a long-haired blonde dog living with me, I've had to become much more relaxed about it. I'd have to attach a vacuum to her behind, and since Maxine thinks the Dyson is a monster that wants to kill her...well you can see my problem! Do you have pets? I've been told I do not snore. I'm a side sleeper. I'm not a very good cook. Hmm, let me rephrase that. I wouldn't say I like to cook, so I don't try to make big fancy meals. I work a lot. It can be challenging with friends and a partner. The people in my inner circle must be very understanding. I've had a partner who didn't quite understand. I'm a Libra and close to all Libra traits. They say Libra has a hard time making decisions, which is certainly not an issue for me. I'm emotional and not afraid to be either. Tears come easily at times of sadness, anger, happiness, love, etc. I like holding hands. Tonight, I get to stay home! Just a little bit of work, but most of the evening, my little behind will be on the couch watching Netflix. I can't wait! I hope you had a good day!*

After messaging for a few weeks, Cara was ready to meet. Even though rejection would feel once again like she wasn't good enough, she knew it was time to make the step. So, when Natasha replied that she would like to meet, all Cara felt was pride in herself.

CHAPTER 26

Dating Natasha

It was a sunny Sunday afternoon and Cara was meeting Natasha today for the first time at a central coffee shop in Glenmore Landing. Cara was feeling excited but also a little nervous. She felt comfortable knowing as much as she did about Natasha but meeting her was something completely different. Cara pulled into the parking lot early and waited in her car until she saw her walk up to the coffee shop doors.

What if Natasha has a strong French accent, and I can't understand her? She'd said she had a French background. What if she's nothing like she portrayed in their conversations? If that's the case, how do I end the meetup?

With sweaty pits, Cara breathed in and out three times, trying to push aside all her nervousness, thankful she had slathered on extra deodorant that morning. She decided to go in with an open mind and let the cards fall where they may.

Natasha's piercing green eyes caught Cara's attention right off the bat, and the fact that she smelled so good was just a bonus.

Cara held Natasha's gaze as she extended her hand. "Hi," she said, smiling from ear to ear. "I'm Cara."

"It's so nice to meet you in person, finally."

No accent, *phew*, and her handshake was strong but not overbearing. She was confident.

When they got to the till to pay for their drinks, Natasha leaned in with her bank card. "I got this!"

Seeing her jump in and pay was refreshing. "Thanks for the tea, Natasha."

"There's a table for two on the patio…it's positioned perfectly for a bit of privacy for our conversation."

Cara was relieved when Natasha lowered her volume as she started asking Cara questions. Cara was not out to the world, and it felt good knowing Natasha respected her privacy. Cara studied her while she spoke, to see if this was someone she could become attracted to. She liked how Natasha presented herself in a short-sleeved soft pink blouse, which was very feminine. Cara guessed she was a bit nervous by how fast she was talking, but that put Cara more at ease, knowing she wasn't the only one. The conversation between the two of them was easy, and an hour passed in a minute.

"I'm enjoying talking with you, Cara. It's such a beautiful day out. Would you be interested in continuing by walking part of the reservoir?"

Cara too was enjoying the visit; a walk sounded perfect. "I'm totally up for that!"

Two and half hours flew by as they talked about anything and everything. When they were back where they had started, Natasha asked Cara if she could walk her to her car.

What a sweet gesture, Cara thought.

Upon reaching Cara's vehicle, they both smiled and shared what a nice time they'd had. As Cara watched Natasha walk away, she thought, *This could have possibilities!*

By the time Cara got home, a text was waiting. Natasha wanted to see Cara again. How great it felt to have someone pursuing her. Cara felt on cloud nine.

Three days later they met for lunch on the corner of Thirty-third and Second Street, where a two-story burgundy house had been converted into a restaurant. They sat at a table toward the back of the room and ordered the fish tacos with the chef's special sauce. The meal was delicious, and the conversation flowed like a river in spring. When finished, they realized that the once-full restaurant was empty, and it was just them left from the lunch crowd.

How easy all of it felt to Cara. They had been laughing and telling stories like they'd known each other forever.

When they walked outside to say their goodbyes, Cara leaned in and hugged her. The soft scent of her perfume and body creams, mixed with the warm feeling Cara felt from the return hug, made Cara notice Natasha on another level. Before driving away, Cara sent a quick text to Natasha, letting her know how much she had enjoyed the embrace.

An instant ping came back: *I enjoyed that hug too!*

Cara planned to kiss Natasha on their third date. Kissing would solidify if there were an actual genuine physical connection. On the third date, they had decided to meet for a drink at a pub in the south end of Calgary. Just like the previous two dates, there were no awkward silences, and the easiness of the conversation helped the connection build. When the bill had been paid and they walked outside to the back of Natasha's car, they shared another heart-fluttering embrace. Cara wanting to explore her feelings a little further jumped into Natasha's passenger seat, leaned in and kissed her.

When their lips parted, Cara could tell immediately that she had caught Natasha off guard because Natasha was stumbling for words. Within seconds, though, she regained her composure, and reached out her hand behind Cara's head, guiding her back in for more. Cara began tingling inside as Natasha's mouth and tongue returned that first kiss with greater urgency. The sexual chemistry was bouncing off the windows.

As the months passed, efforts to set up little get-togethers continued from both sides. For Cara, it felt terrific that Natasha wanted to spend time with her and was excited to see her even after long and busy workdays. She always found time for Cara and it wasn't just Cara trying to make it work; Natasha reciprocated and showed through words and actions that Cara was someone she wanted to be with. Cara had found someone who showed her exactly what she had always thought a relationship was supposed to be like.

CHAPTER 27

She's Back

⚜

C ARA WAS DOING her regular morning treadmill run at the gym, getting her body bikini ready for her trip the next day to Costa Rica with her kids. *This can't be right. I can't believe this.* The hairs on the back of Cara's neck stood at attention. She had been watching a Netflix movie on her phone, something she always did to help pass the time when on the treadmill. Never did she expect to see *her* name pop up in the banner on her phone. Her heart raced as if she had just turned the speed up to ten. Angel Anwir's name was on her screen.

Today, I ran into one of our friends, who said, how's your Cara doing?

Another banner came: *I've been wanting to tell you that I got a promotion at work…my boss said, "Now you can tell Cara."*

And another: *I miss spending time with you. I haven't been enjoying running lately because I need to be doing it with you.*

All those months back, Angel had been crystal clear to Cara, letting her know she wanted nothing to do with her. Now here she was sending text after text, trying to tug at her heartstrings. Cara wanted to ignore the texts, but the pull to reply was too strong: *You were the one who wanted space Angel and didn't want to be with me. Now you have all the time you need to do everything you didn't want to do with me. I'm finally happy again and doing my best to move forward.*

Within seconds, Cara's phone rang. Placing her feet on either side of the running belt, Cara stopped the machine, and in a laboured breath said, "Hello, this is Cara."

"Hi Cara, it's Angel. How have you been?"

Cara's mouth went dry, while her heart jumped up into her throat. *What is happening right now?* "Ahh, I'm doing okay."

"I heard through the grapevine that you and the kids are heading on holiday tomorrow to Costa Rica. I'm so jealous. I would like to meet with you tonight at seven for a send-off drink at the bar side of Charlie's Pizza."

Cara froze. Not able to string together words, her brain went on autopilot. "Sure."

"That's great! I'm looking forward to seeing you, Cara. So much to catch up on."

Immediately with the end of the call, Natasha jumped into Cara's mind. Even though the two of them hadn't gotten to the stage of classifying what they were to each other, feelings were growing, and Cara needed to let her know immediately that she had just agreed to meet up with Angel that night.

※

Cara walked into the bar, unsure of what to expect or how she'd feel or react when she saw *her.*

"Hi Cara, it's so good to see you! You look great."

Even though she had spent so many months trying to bury any feelings bubbling beneath the surface, nothing could prepare her for what she felt when she saw Angel. She looked stunning… and those dimples, those dimples had always melted Cara. Sitting across from her was the woman who still held her heart.

As the minutes passed to hours, Cara found herself falling right back into their natural rhythm. The conversation was easy like always, unforced like they had never been apart. Glancing at her watch, Cara realized almost three hours had passed. "I need to get going, Angel; I have an eleven a.m. flight tomorrow."

Just before getting into their cars, Angel leaned in and hugged her goodbye. "I hope you have an amazing trip, Cara!"

Before Cara could say thanks, Angel kissed her on the mouth. Cara immediately pulled back, shocked. "I have to go, Angel; thanks for the wings and drinks."

Driving home, Cara shook her head back and forth to what had just transpired. *Why does Angel feel she can just waltz back into my life. She didn't even apologize tonight for how she treated me when she'd crushed me like a bug on the bottom of her shoe. Just when I'm finally getting my life back on track, here she comes strolling back in like she'd never broken up with me. I can't lie, it was nice to see her but I can't believe she kissed me!*

—※—

Texts from Angel during the holiday continued daily.
I hope you're having fun!
The pictures look great on Facebook; so jealous.
What are you up to today?
What is the temperature there?

Cara replied to a couple of her texts, but mostly she ignored them until she received one that said, *I saw on Facebook you're coming home tomorrow. Can we meet up that night?*

Cara had zero interest in meeting up with Angel; she was excited to get back and spend time with Natasha and had no intention of seeing Angel. *That's not possible, Angel; I have plans.*

How about the day after? I have something important I need to talk to you about.

I might be able to meet you then, but I'll have to get back to you on that.

As soon as the plane landed and Cara had dropped her kids off at home, she drove to see Natasha. The excitement inside was building the closer she got. Before Natasha's door fully closed behind Cara, she had Natasha wrapped in her arms, kissing her deeply.

"Before we go any further, I want to share something with you. Angel sent me texts while I was away." Cara took the time to let Natasha see all the texts, Angel had sent. "As you can see, she's asked to meet up with me tomorrow."

Natasha took hold of Cara's hands, "Just remember, I have feelings too. I've missed you, Cara, but if your heart is being pulled in another direction, I need you to figure that out before we go any further."

Cara hadn't brought on any of Angel's advances, but she knew Natasha was right. It wasn't fair to her that Cara was even talking to Angel. She needed to figure things out and fast. "This isn't how I had hoped our evening would go, Natasha, but I completely understand where you're coming from. I'll meet with Angel tomorrow to hear what she has to say and to let her know I'm seeing you."

The King Henry was a bar in Okotoks. The high coffered ceilings, wood panelling and trim gave it a substantial English pub feel. A large bar in the middle separated the restaurant from the pub side where they had planned to meet. The establishment had great food and atmosphere, and except for the odd weekend when a live band was brought in, the place was quiet enough to afford a good space to visit and talk.

As soon as they both were seated and a drink ordered, Angel got right to her point. "Cara, I don't want to give up on our relationship anymore, and I am willing to change to save what we once had. In the past, I was lazy in our relationship. I would regularly use being tired or not feeling well as an excuse not to see you. Even though I knew how important time with me was to you, I would cancel plans last minute because it made me feel in control."

Cara couldn't believe what Angel was saying out loud.

"I want that all to change, and from now on, when I say I'm going to do something with you, I'm going to follow through and not just say it. I want to start fresh and am now willing to tell my kids and anyone else, so the relationship won't be a secret this time. I *promise*, Cara, you will not regret it."

Cara sat back in her chair. Hearing the word 'promise' struck a chord with her. This was what she had always wished for from Angel, but it was no longer just the two of them in this scenario. Cara took in a deep breath. "Someone else is part of this equation now, Angel, and it's not as simple as me just saying, sure, let's try again."

"Don't give up on me for a short relationship you have started with someone else. Do you love this person?"

Cara immediately knew the answer. She cared deeply for Natasha, but she hadn't allowed herself to fully open her heart again to say those three words. "I'm not in love, but our relationship has grown, and I care for her." Angel just stared at Cara, but Cara wasn't about to give Angel an answer right then and there from the bomb she had just exploded on her. "This is a lot, Angel. I need time to process this. I'm not going to stay for the drink, I need to go now and figure this all out."

CHAPTER 28

Opening Up

~~~

CARA LAY RESTLESS in bed as a snowstorm whirled outside her bedroom window. She felt mentally exhausted even though she was just waking up. Her night had been filled with interrupted sleep, plagued with unsure thoughts. She *wants me back, Mom. She even said she'll tell her kids about us. She used the most sacred word to me, 'promise'. She's disappointed me so many times that I'm not sure if I should believe her. Do I give her another chance?*

Cara knew, that now was the time she needed to let Lila know about her and Angel's past romantic relationship. She was nervous about Lila's reaction, but she needed someone to talk to who could answer back, and Lila was her Person. She didn't think it was fair to blindside her with a phone call, so she sat up in bed and wrote her a text. The fear of losing Lila had Cara's stomach in knots. The thought of throwing up was in the forefront of her mind as she held her thumb over the send button. *Do I, do it? I can't keep this secret any longer.* She hit send.

No more than fifteen minutes later, her phone rang, with Lila on the other end.

"Cara, thank you for sharing this important part of your life with me. It doesn't matter who you love; all that matters to me is that you're happy."

The weight of a thousand cruise ships fell from Cara's shoulders. "Seriously, you're okay with it?" Cara asked as she quietly exhaled.

"Of course, I am, Cara. I saw a few things that made me think something might be going on with you two, but I wasn't going to say anything until it came from you."

"And here I thought we had been very discreet."

"The hot tub party at your place felt a little off when I walked up to you two in the tub. I also saw you and Angel hugging one time. You both held on longer than just friends hugging."

"I can't get much past you, Lila," Cara giggled with embarrassment.

"I do have some questions, though."

"Ask away."

"Did you always know you liked women?"

"These feelings began with Angel, Lila. It wasn't something I grew up feeling or questioned myself about when I was younger. It was something Angel and I just fell into, and it felt right."

"Why did you decide to share this now?"

Cara filled Lila in on the hurtful breakup and the situation she was now faced with.

"OMG, Cara, I'm so sorry you had to go through that breakup alone. If I'd known, I would've been there for you."

"I know you would have, Lila. I wish I'd shared all this with you when I first had feelings for her, but it wasn't the right time. The problem now is that I'm not sure what to do. Natasha is lovely, Lila, but my heart is still tied to Angel."

"I can't tell you what to do, but you might want to think about holding off going back to Angel and see where things go with Natasha. What's meant for you won't go past you. If Angel means what she says, she will wait for you; if she doesn't, you two were never meant to be."

"I appreciate everything you've said, Lila, and thank you for listening and being here for me. I need some time now to think all this over and figure out what I'm going to do."

"Cara, we are always just one decision away from changing our entire lives."

CHAPTER 29

Goodbye

How do you tell someone you care about them but can't be with them? How do you take care of your wants and needs knowing that at the same time, you're going to hurt someone? The decision weighed heavy on Cara. What if she was making the biggest mistake of her life?

Cara had arranged to meet Natasha at her house. As hard as it was, she gave Natasha the letter that she had painstakingly written, hoping she had explained everything clearly and gently.

Natasha, getting to know you has been one of the best things in my life. You have shown me that what I am looking for in a relationship is out there. You have shown me, not only with words but also with your actions, how you truly care and feel about me. There is nothing phony about you, and I so appreciate that. You are open to sharing what you want and need, something that does not come easy to me, but I am constantly working on improving. There is no guessing with you, Natasha! You say exactly what you mean. There has never been a doubt that when you say you are completely committed, I believe you because you are such a truthful and honest person. It is something you should never change about yourself because it is such a special and unique quality. Even though I am a very private person who keeps so much close to my heart, you have made me feel comfortable enough to share some of my wants and needs without ever feeling judged or worried that you will take it negatively. You have taught me in such a short time to honour all I have to offer and be comfortable with who I am becoming. I have truly enjoyed every moment spent with you. Everything I have said to you has come from my heart and has been honest and true. That is why I need to say this to you now. I cannot say I love you because even though I want to, my heart is not a hundred percent there. From the beginning, you told me you are looking for that forever love, someone you can share your life with and who will be committed to you the way you will be committed to them. I so wanted to be the one to give that to you, but I know that at this time, I cannot promise that. My heart is still being pulled in another direction, which is not allowing me to commit a hundred percent to you. It breaks my heart to say this, but I must end what I have started with you. Please know that I care for you and this decision was difficult.

Placing the letter in her lap, Natasha took a moment before expressing her thoughts. "I felt something was off, Cara, when you returned from holiday and even though this was tough to read, I understand and appreciate your honesty. I wish things could have been different, but I hope things work out for you."

Driving home, Cara thought, *"What a classy woman."* Cara would be forever grateful for what the two of them had shared. Natasha had taught her what a healthy relationship looked like, and Cara's only wish was that Natasha would one day find that special someone who would love her even more profoundly than the love Natasha was able to give.

CHAPTER 30
Telling the Kids

~~~

Cara honestly didn't know how her kids would react to the news that their mom was in love with a woman. Cody was turning eleven next month and Dani would be thirteen in January, so they were old enough to understand love is love, but this was something much closer to home. They knew Angel as part of their mom's friend group, but finding out now, that she is their mom's partner was something Cara wasn't sure they would accept.

Cara had raised her kids to be inclusive of others. She'd even shared personal stories with them, like the one about little Billy Evans in high school and Sven Stevenson in university, to show them how being kind and accepting can impact someone's life.

Billy was a boy who kept to himself. His head was always down as he walked through the halls, with greasy hair and unkempt T-shirts that always looked one size too small. Due to his nerdy nature, he was constantly bullied by the older boys. If Cara was around when the name-calling or harassing occurred, she never had an issue walking right up to the kids doing the bullying and saying to them, "How would you like it if you were walking down the hall and I started saying those mean things to you?" She wasn't afraid to stand up to them and truly felt sad for any kids being intimidated. Billy had barely looked at Cara, let alone spoken to her during their four years in high school, but that changed on the last day of school in the spring of 1985. Billy walked right up to Cara and handed her a card. In the softest whisper, he said, "Thank you," his eyes locking onto hers for barely a millisecond before he quickly shuffled away. He wrote in the card, *Thank you, Cara, for being the one person in high school who stood up for me. You made coming to school a little easier.* And at the very bottom, he'd drawn a little red heart.

That had been the first time in Cara's life she'd realized the effect you could have on someone by supporting them and using kindness. She'd shared that story with her kids hoping it would impact them. She'd had a similar experience in university that she felt was essential to pass on to her kids too. She was at an introduction party for all first-year students in her course. She was mingling with a group of kids she had just met when out of the corner of her eye, she saw an adult student sitting by himself a few tables over. Cara, without even thinking, walked over to him, introduced herself, and asked if he would like to join the group.

One week before graduation, Sven Stevenson came to Cara's house, something he had never done before. He had come to her place that day to thank her personally. He told her that because of her one simple act of kindness four years earlier, he had made fantastic friends from that group, giving him so many great memories of his time in university.

Cara knew these stories impacted Dani because she, like Cara, stood up for others who may not have had a strong voice. Dani was confident in showing her support toward the LGBTQ+ kids in her Catholic school, having no issues whatsoever facing both students and teachers who were homophobic. Cara had always been so proud of her convictions, and even though she wasn't sure how Dani would react to the news, she felt she should tell her first.

Finding Dani in her bedroom, Cara paused, drew in a deep breath, and started the conversation. "You know how I told you you'd never have to worry about getting a new Dad. Well, you won't ever have to worry about that because I've fallen in love with a woman."

The first word out of Dani's mouth was, "Yes!" Followed by pumping her fists toward the ceiling with a big smile on her face.

Cara smiled. All her worry about the possibility that Dani would not be too thrilled or accepting of the news had been washed away in a split second. "Angel and I have fallen in love, and we no longer want to keep it a secret. By your reaction, I can see you are okay with it. Honestly, I was a little worried you might not be."

"Of course, I'm okay with it, Mom! I'm a bit hurt that you thought I might not be."

"I'm not sure how anyone will react to this news, Dani, but as long as you and Cody are good with it, it won't matter to me now what anyone else thinks."

"Do Ella and Jayden know?"

"Angel is talking to her girls tonight."

"Can I tell my friends?"

"I'm a private person, Dani, but if you need to tell your close friends, I'm okay with it. Let's just give Angel time to tell her girls before anyone else finds out."

"That makes sense."

"If you are all good, Dani, I want to talk to Cody now."

"All good, Momma!"

Cara walked across the hall to Cody's room and found him playing one of his computer games. Feeling relieved from sharing the news with Dani, she was ready for the same conversation with Cody. "Hey, my boy, can I talk to you for a moment?"

Pulling off his headset, "Sure, Mom, what's up?"

"I just shared something with Dani that I now want to share with you."

Cody looked at his mom with uncertainty in his eyes.

"You know how I told you you'd never have to worry about getting a new dad? Well, I have fallen in love with a—"

"I knew you would find a guy—"

"...woman."

"Wait, *what?*"

"No, you go ahead."

"No, you finish what you were saying, Mom."

"I've fallen in love with Angel."

Turning his gaming chair to face his mom, Cody said, "I always thought you would meet a man, Mom, but it's no big deal to me that it's a woman. Since it's Angel, that's cool with me. I'm happy for you."

"I honestly wasn't sure if you and Dani would be okay with this news, but Dani's all good with it too!"

"Mom, if Dani or I were gay, would you still love us?"

"Of course, I would."

"Then why would you think we would feel any differently about you loving Angel?"

"You kids amaze me." Leaning down she gave Cody a gigantic mom hug.

Cara's love at that moment toward her two kids quadrupled. All that was important to them was that she was happy. She had never wanted to keep secrets from them, so finally, sharing this special and important part of her life felt spectacular. She let out an enormous sigh as she walked back upstairs, grateful for her children's love and acceptance. Though her secret was out, she wasn't planning on running to the rooftops yelling *I'm in love with a woman*, but no longer would she live with the worry of others finding out.

CHAPTER 31

Hiccups in the Road

~~~

"Hey, Cara, thanks for coming to my place for tea tonight."

"Thanks for the invite, Angel."

"I wanted to let you know that when I drove my girls to school this morning, Jayden told me she overheard Dani's best friend Trish telling some other kids at school about us."

Cara's stomach tightened with thoughts of how Angel might react to what was shared. "Are you okay with that, Angel?"

"I'm completely fine with it, and when I asked the girls, they had no issues either."

Cara breathed more easily. "Well, that's good news. I'm so glad everything's been going well with both our families since we told them."

Cara was grateful their relationship had been running smoothly. It had only been a couple of months since they had shared everything with their kids, but life was good. They had been spending lots of time together going for walks, out for a drink, or just doing simple things like sharing tea or watching a movie at one another's homes. Spending every second weekend together had been a priority for them both now so their connection was getting stronger all the time. There had been some ups and downs, but overall they were like an average couple now enjoying just being their true selves.

"Are we going to spend this weekend at your place, Cara?"

"I'd like that. I can't believe how cold it's been, so instead of us going out anywhere, would you be good with me cooking that hardy chicken dinner with mayo you like so much for tomorrow night, and maybe we can order a pizza for Saturday supper and just make it a Netflix in bed weekend."

"Yes, and Yum! That all sounds great. Can't wait!"

≈

That weekend, with their stomachs full from Cara's chicken recipe, they cuddled in bed, letting their bellies settle while watching a comedy movie.

Ring...

"Sorry, I thought I had turned my ringer off."

"No worries, Cara; looks like it's Dani."

"Hey, my girl, what's up?"

"I'm feeling anxious tonight, Mom. I want Trish to stay over with me, but Dad keeps saying no. I want to come back home tonight with her. Can I please?"

Cara remembered being told by Cody earlier that week that their dad wanted to spend more time doing things with Dani and him on the weekends when they were at his place, so

Cara thought this was probably why Jay was saying no to Dani. "Maybe Dad just wants to hang out with you, Dani, and not your friends."

"He's not spending time with me, Mom; he's upstairs drinking, and I want to have Trish stay with me."

Cara remembered being thirteen. It's such an emotional time for girls and boys. "Let me chat with your dad." While she waited for Jay, she looked over at Angel, mouthing, *Sorry*. Angel had been snuggled in close, so Cara was pretty sure she had overheard what Dani was saying.

"Hey, Jay Dani would like to have Trish stay with her tonight. Is that an issue?"

When Angel heard Jay's voice, she let go of Cara's arm and slid over to her side of the bed.

"I'm tired of her always having friends over on our weekends together. I'd like to start having those weekends with just her and Cody."

"I hear you, Jay. She's pretty upset. She said you're drinking and not spending time with her, so she just wants to come back home and stay here tonight."

"I've had one beer, Cara, while I'm watching the 8 o'clock news. I was giving Dani time to have fun with her friend and then I was planning on spending the rest of the evening playing some board games with her and Cody. She's all emotional now crying downstairs, so I'm just going to drop her off at your place and I'll try again tomorrow."

Cara whispered to Angel, "Is it okay if the two girls come back here for just tonight?"

"Of course, that's okay!" Pulling the blankets tight under her arms.

Jay was at the door about thirty minutes later. After getting them settled away downstairs in Dani's bedroom, she climbed back into bed with Angel. The mood in the room had done a one-eighty. The laughing, cuddling, upbeat time they had been having before the girls arrived, had now turned quiet and cold.

"Cara, since Dani has Trish over, I don't like the idea of being in bed with you."

"Please don't feel that way, Angel. The kids know you are here and you and I have had this conversation and agreed that it's okay to sleep at each other's homes when our kids are there."

"I just don't feel comfortable."

The last thing Cara wanted was for Angel to feel uncomfortable. "No worries, I'll sleep on the couch."

Before grabbing a pillow and blanket from the closet, Cara playfully hugged and kissed Angel, wishing her sweet dreams as she quietly closed the bedroom door and made her way to the living room.

In the morning, Cara prepared thick pancakes loaded with melted butter and syrup before singing out to Angel that breakfast was ready. Angel entered the kitchen and without saying a word, Cara felt something was off. "What's wrong, Angel?"

"I'm upset that you allowed Dani to be driven home by Jay last night when you knew he'd been drinking."

"What? When I spoke to Jay last night, he told me he'd only had a beer and he didn't sound drunk on the phone. Even when he dropped the girls off, he certainly didn't give me any impression that he was the least bit tipsy. You know how kids are, Angel, they exaggerate sometimes when they want something. If I had thought for a second Jay had been drunk when I was on the phone with him, I would have gone and picked the girls up myself. I thought you were upset last night because Dani's friend was over."

"I don't like how everything happened. I'm going to head home now."

Cara was caught off guard by Angel's comment and reaction. "Can we talk about this, Angel?"

"I just want to go home, Cara."

Cara knew that leaving things in a bad state without discussing it, had not worked well for them in the past. "When things like this come up, Angel, we should talk it through, so we know where each other's head is."

"If you don't want this weekend to spiral any worse, you should just let this go."

Billions of needles prickled all over Cara's body. "Please call me later, Angel, so I know everything is okay."

At the door, Angel's hug goodbye was quick.

Cara tried to make sense of everything that had happened. *Last night, Angel said she was upset and uncomfortable because Dani's friend had been there, and now this morning, she's upset with me for something that's not even true. Why did she change her story this morning? It's almost as if Angel realized her reaction last night was not fair to me and now, she needed a different excuse so she could blame me for last night's event.* Cara didn't want to make it a bigger deal than it was, so she calmed her thoughts, thinking there would always be hiccups here and there in their relationship, so hopefully, this incident was just one of those hiccups that wouldn't amount to anything.

CHAPTER 32

A Night Out That Ends Badly

❧

"The Tavern sure is busy tonight, Angel."
"It's probably because everyone is tired of hibernating."
"Yes, that makes sense. What time is your sister Liz joining us?"
"She's walking through the doors right now."

"Hello, ladies!" Even though Liz had been living in Calgary for almost thirty years, she still held onto her English accent from spending the first part of her life living in England. Angel and Cara always giggled when she'd say *I can't do* something because it always sounded like she was saying *I cunt do this*. Cara liked Liz. She had always made Cara feel like part of the family, including Cara if she hosted a party with her husband, Dan, or an evening out with her friends.

Just as Liz was about to sit across from Cara and Angel, the waitress placed two drinks on the table that neither Cara nor Angel had ordered.

"These drinks are from the two guys sitting over there at the edge of the dance floor."

"Love it when I get a free drink." Looking at the two guys, Angel raised her drink and mouthed, "Thanks."

"Let's buy them a drink back, Angel, so we're even, and then they won't expect anything from us."

"I think that would be a smart move, ladies," Liz said, as she ordered a drink.

The music started pumping and a large group of women filled the dance floor. A couple of them, Cara knew. "You should go dance with them, Cara. You love dancing," Angel said.

While she stroked Angel's leg under the table, she said, "I'm good sitting right here with you and Liz."

The night progressed and more drinks were had, with Angel being persistent in trying to get Cara to go dance. "I see you moving in your seat, Cara. Go dance, you'll have fun."

"Look, Angel, I'll go up if you come too."

"I suck at dancing. Look the ladies are back up and they keep looking over here…go dance with them."

Cara turned and as soon as her friends saw her looking, they waved at her to come on the dance floor.

"Go on, dance with them."

"Are you sure you won't come dance with me, Angel?"

"I'm sure."

"Okay then, I'll just dance to a couple of songs and be right back."

Cara was having a blast busting out her best dance moves and laughing with the other ladies. When the second song finished and she spun toward Angel and Liz, she noticed that one of the guys who had bought them a drink earlier was now standing at the edge of their table talking with Angel.

As Cara approached the table she said, "Now that was fun," positioning herself back in her seat.

Angel just ignored Cara and continued her conversation with the guy. She didn't acknowledge nor introduce her. She just kept talking to him with her back to Cara.

Liz must have felt Cara's awkwardness about what was happening right in front of her face and said, "It looked like you were having a great time out there, Cara."

Cara gave Liz a half smile, then sat staring at Angel's back. She waited patiently while Angel and the guy did a couple of tequila shots. Cara had had enough and tapped Angel on the shoulder whispering in her ear, "Hey, I'm sitting right here. Do you think you could turn back to me now?"

With a snarky look on her face, Angel said, "No, I'm good," before getting up from her seat, grabbing the guy's hand and taking him on the dance floor.

Cara's mouth dropped open, followed by the feeling of her blood boiling through her veins. She leaned across the table to Liz, "This is bullshit!"

"Angel's never been one to hold her liquor well, Cara."

"That doesn't mean it's okay, Liz. Doing this is so disrespectful to me."

"As soon as the song is over, I'll get her, Cara."

"Whatever Liz, I'm out of here." Cara grabbed her jacket, paid her bill and made a beeline to the door.

The next day, Cara's phone rang around noon.

"Hey, thanks for getting me so drunk last night and leaving me there," Angel said.

"Um, you can thank the guy who kept buying you shots for why you were so drunk last night, not me, and I left because you were ignoring me and being extremely disrespectful."

"Liz told me she and I left right after you. On our walk back to my place, I wiped out and ripped open my knee. It hurts like hell today."

Cara continued listening to Angel ramble on, waiting for an apology that never came.

CHAPTER 33

A Little Wiser

~

Cara was passing time enjoying a walk around Okotoks admiring all the pink and white cherry blossom trees that were now in full bloom, knowing the flowers would fall as quickly as they had shown up. It was her weekend with Angel, so she was waiting to hear from her to know what time they were going to meet after Angel finished work at five. Cara's spirits were high with the warmth of the sun on her face under clear blue skies.

Bing went off Cara's phone: *Hi Cara, the kids won't be spending this weekend at their dad's as planned, so our plans together are going to change.*

Since Cara didn't know exactly what Angel's text meant, she called for clarification. "Hi, Angel."

"Hello."

"Just calling to see what our weekend will look like with your kids being home."

"Let's still hang out this evening and during the day Saturday and Sunday, but I'm not going to have you stay over tonight or tomorrow night."

"Don't get me wrong, Angel, I'm glad we're still hanging out during the day, but why do our night plans need to change?"

"Let me call you right back, Cara; I'd like to talk with my kids first."

"Sounds good." Cara started making her way back to where she had parked her car.

Ring…Angel's name came up on her screen.

"Hello there. So, what's the plan?" Excited that she would soon be seeing Angel.

"I've decided to spend the entire weekend with the girls now; let's just get together next week."

Cara's high spirits instantly took a nosedive. Those unwanted familiar feelings bubbled in her stomach with Angel making decisions that didn't include Cara being part of the conversation. Cara didn't want to make a big deal of it though, so instead of saying how she felt, she just agreed with it all and hung up.

Cara knew the best way to keep the relationship running smoothly, was to just go along with Angel. It sucked that she still didn't feel a hundred percent safe to freely communicate her thoughts mainly due to comments from Angel like, 'You're treating me like a child by repeating what we've already discussed', or 'As long as your needs are being met, then you're happy,' or 'You make our relationship all about you'. Those experiences had Cara holding her tongue at times rather than communicating how she felt.

Cara decided to give Lila a call. "Hey Lila, would you be up for a tea visit this evening?"

"You bet. Will Angel and Sophie be joining us?"

"No, it's just going to be you and me."

"Great! It will give us a chance to get caught up on things. Why don't you swing by my place around six thirty? I'll make us some supper to go along with that tea."

"That sounds fabulous, Lila. See you soon."

Since she'd now made plans with Lila, like always, she wanted to keep Angel in the loop so she sent her a quick text. *Hey, Angel, just letting you know since we're not getting together tonight, I'm going to hang out at Lila's place for a visit.*

Instant reply: *I wish you were okay staying home when we aren't together. I know you don't like being alone, but I love staying home alone. You should be more like that.*

Hearing the person who is supposed to love and support her say that comment, made Cara question her decision to still go out. *Maybe I need to get more comfortable with staying home by myself. Am I wrong to want to go out with friends when Angel doesn't want to spend time with me?* Cara shook those thoughts away. Getting in her car, she drove home first to change out of her workout pants and into some jeans and a fresh shirt before making her way to Lila's house.

"Being in your home Lila, always puts me in such a peaceful state."

"Well, I'm happy to hear that," she smiled as she topped up Cara's teacup. "So, what's been happening in the life of Cara?"

"Where do I start…"

"Give me the scoop."

"I'm so confused, Lila. I need to know your thoughts." Cara exhaled deeply, then filled Lila in on the weekend Dani had come home, the issue at the bar and her conversation with Angel today.

"Wow! I hope you don't get mad at me for saying this, Cara, but Angel has a lot of characteristics of a narcissist."

"A narcissist? I don't even know what that is."

"This is so crazy that you're telling me all this today, because last night, I was watching a recorded *Dr. Phil* episode that talked in detail about narcissism. You need to check out his podcast on covert narcissists because I swear Angel has so many characteristics."

"Covert narcissist?"

"It's a person who manipulates and controls their partner, making them feel like it's their fault for all the problems in their relationship."

"Seriously?"

"You know how Angel tells you she wants time to herself after you guys have had an argument that hasn't been resolved?"

"Yes."

"And then she goes silent for days or weeks while you beat yourself up trying to figure out if you did something wrong?"

"Yes."

"A covert narcissist will test you through silent treatment. They will stay silent and ignore you in the hope that by not talking to you for a while, the issue that caused them to go silent won't get discussed, so they can get away with whatever they did wrong. It's a tactic they use."

"What? I didn't even know that was a thing!"

"It's how they control people."

"Lila, Angel once told me that there were times, she would choose not to spend time with me even if she had nothing to do. She would lie to me, telling me she was too tired or didn't feel well. Who does that to someone they're supposed to love?"

"Ah, a covert narcissist."

"This is blowing my mind, Lila."

"Even the comment she made to you today, wishing you would be okay staying home when you aren't together—that's passive-aggressive, Cara. She's trying to manipulate you to do what she thinks you should or shouldn't do."

Cara shook her head, trying to process everything Lila was saying. She had never looked at what Angel had been doing in this way; this information was not even in her wheelhouse.

"It's not okay what she's been doing to you, and don't let her make you think you're wrong for telling her how you feel; that's called healthy communication. What you need to stop doing is allowing her to treat you this way."

"I feel stupid now!"

"Don't feel that way, Cara. You love Angel and want the relationship to work, so you're doing whatever it takes to make that happen. What's wrong is Angel thinking it's okay to disrespect you, and then blaming you for your reaction. Kinda like the way she did to you with that guy in the bar."

"Lila, you have no idea how many times I've walked away from conversations with Angel, wishing I had never even brought it up due to the outcome. She is so good at spinning the conversation to make it look like I'm always the problem. Do you know she convinced me once that I was the reason for her feeling sick? I felt so bad about it that I apologized to her. How brutal is that? I swear the only time she accepts responsibility for her actions or non-action is whenever she wants me back."

"She's manipulating you, Cara. I'm just going to go grab my phone from my purse and google covert narcissist."

Cara sat back in the chair trying to process everything Lila had just shared.

'I just googled it. It says they blame, shame, and ignore the feelings and needs of other people."

"OMG, Lila, I just realized she doesn't just do this to me. I never told you this, but she feels good about making people cry at work!"

"That's messed up, Cara. Why do you stay in the relationship with her?"

"I truly do love her, Lila. When the relationship is going well, it's great, and when it gets bad, I'm always hopeful it will return to the way it was in the beginning. I believe her every time she says she sees the two of us together forever and that she loves me. I don't want to be alone, Lila."

"I get that, but when she's treating you poorly, how do you feel then?"

"Mostly I feel very confused, unimportant to her, like what I say doesn't matter."

"What she's doing is not love, Cara."

CHAPTER 34

Christmas and New Years

CARA FELT WARM and cozy with the heat of the fireplace against her back as she sat on the living room floor wrapping the last of the Christmas presents. She couldn't believe how quickly the year had come and gone. Glancing up, she saw the havoc that old man winter was causing outside. The wind was blowing a gale throwing millions of snowflakes left then right as she curled the strings of red ribbon with the edge of her scissors. She hoped Dani would be excited Christmas Eve for the pair of white canvas Converse high tops that were now hidden in a box beneath the shiny silver wrapping paper. The view stirred up dread that soon she would have to leave the comfort of her home to pick the kids up from school. Where had the day gone? It was already 3:05 p.m.

Ring...

"Hello, this is Cara."

"Hey Cara, I'm sorry I've been so distant lately. I'm missing you."

"That's okay Angel. It's a busy time of year."

"It's no excuse, from now on, when you see me doing this, point it out to me because sometimes I don't realize I'm even doing it."

"Sounds good, I'll do that."

"Since you don't have your kids Christmas day, I would love for you to join me and my family at my sister's next Saturday for Christmas dinner."

"I would love that. Thanks for the invite."

"The dinner is going to be around six thirty. The only thing I need to figure out is how we're all going to get there."

"I could pick your mom up on the way to help you out. Having the company for the long drive to northeast Calgary would be nice. The news forecast has been calling for a big storm Christmas night too, so it would be great not to drive by myself."

"We'll figure something out. We've got some time."

Twice that week, Cara followed up with Angel asking if the ride situation had been worked out, but all Angel told her each time was, "We'll figure it out."

After Dani and Cody left to spend Christmas day and night with their dad, Cara decided to finish up the last bit of accounting work on her desk. When she came across the receipt Angel had been asking for earlier in the week for the gift Cara had picked up on Angel's behalf for Liz, she sent a quick text letting Angel know the amount.

Angel replied: *How can you be texting me asking for money when I'm so stressed out from my work week and trying to get ready for the Christmas dinner?*

Not expecting that reply, Cara called Angel. "Hey Angel, I was finishing up some of my accounting work when I came across the receipt you had asked me for. That is why I sent you the text."

"I can't deal with that right now. I'm trying to get ready, and I'm scheduling pickups to get everyone to the party."

"No worries; there's no rush to send the money. So, what's the plan for tonight? Will I be taking your mom?"

"My mom wants to drive with me."

"How about I pick up Justin to come with me?"

"I want all my kids in my car due to the big storm tonight."

Cara's heart sank. Why wasn't Angel thinking about her having to drive alone in the snowstorm? Cara could understand Angel wanting to have her younger daughters with her, but her son was in his twenties, and Cara got along great with him. Surely, he could have driven up with her. "Um, okay. I didn't think I would be driving alone in the snowstorm, especially when you said all week that you would figure it out, but I guess I am. See you later, Angel."

On the drive up, Cara decided she wasn't going to let her evening be ruined by being upset about the driving situation. So, when Liz met her at the door, Cara had a big smile on her face. She was a little nervous having to face Angel, afraid that her emotions might get the best of her, but when Angel met her at the top of the stairs embracing Cara with a calming hug and whispering into her ear, 'I'm so glad you made it here safely,' followed by, 'What can I get you to drink?' Cara's reservations disappeared.

Christmas music, laughter and freshly roasted turkey filled the house. Wearing the coloured tissue paper crowns freshly popped from the Christmas Crackers while they gathered around the dining table giggling at the silly jokes that came with the cheesy prizes within, had Cara in the best of Christmas spirits that evening. Enjoying not only one but two helpings of turkey with mashed potatoes, roasted carrots, and freshly baked buns, Cara noticed the satisfied look on Liz's face as Cara joined them back at the table with her second filled dish. After everyone looked as if they couldn't put one more piece of anything into their mouths, Cara jumped up to help clear the dishes from the table before filling the dishwasher so that the cook didn't have to clean up too. It was almost 11 p.m. when yawns passed around the room. Getting up from the couch where she had been snuggling beside Angel, Cara walked around the living room giving everyone a hug goodbye and sharing, "This tired gal is heading home now." After thanking Liz for hosting such a wonderful Christmas Eve, Cara hugged Angel at the top of the foyer stairs before making her way down to get her boots and coat on.

"Any chance I could get a ride home with you, Cara?" Justin asked.

Happy for the company, she gladly said, "Of course!"

Angel immediately said, "Are you sure you don't want to come with us?"

In disbelief, Cara stood there with a shocked look on her face.

"All good, Mom. I'll go home with Cara."

"Are you sure, Justin?"

"Ah, ya Mom, all good."

Cara noticed the nervous look on Angel's face from Justin's reply. Was Angel worried Cara might say something to him about the ride situation? Cara knew that conversation was between her and Angel, a conversation she would be having with Angel tomorrow.

The next morning, as soon as Cara woke up, she called Angel. "Hey, Angel!"

"Good morning, Cara!"

"I wanted to let you know that I had a great time at dinner yesterday, but I did want to talk about how I felt regarding the driving situation."

"What do you mean?"

"I tried more than once this past week to talk with you about having someone drive with me and it wasn't until the night of that you informed me I would be driving alone. You made the carpooling decision without asking me how I felt about driving by myself in that weather. I'm your partner, Angel, and the situation I was left in yesterday hurt."

"Why didn't you pull me aside at the party and tell me how you felt?"

"I'm telling you now, as I would have been too emotional to have pulled you aside at the party and tried to explain how I was feeling."

"You know, Cara, I'm not sure if our relationship is worth it."

Cara froze. Angel's automatic reaction whenever Cara voiced her feelings was to throw in the towel. All Cara wanted was for Angel to hear what she was sharing with her instead of having Angel ignore her concerns. Instantly, Cara regretted saying how she felt, but she wanted to explain herself so maybe Angel would understand. "Hey Angel, when I point something out in a discussion with you about how something you do makes me feel, I'm not trying to make you feel bad or saying it to end us. I'm saying it so you will hear how certain things you do affect me and make me feel. Just because you don't feel the same, doesn't make my feelings unjustified. You and I are two different people, and we have different needs. Being open and communicating those needs should keep our relationship strong, not tear it apart. When I bring things up to you, and your first reply is, 'I'm not sure our relationship is worth it,' those words cut like a knife and make me feel very insecure about us. I shouldn't have to feel that you will leave me whenever I want to talk to you about my feelings."

"It wasn't fair to you that you had to drive to the party alone, Cara. I wanted to go with you, but I had my whole family to worry about. I knew you were hurt by it, and I'm sorry."

"This is all I am asking for, Angel. For you to recognize and understand how certain things you choose to do without making me a part of the decision process affects me. I want us to discuss things together. Thanks for hearing me; that makes me feel a lot better."

The snow was softly falling from the night sky as Cara and Angel walked along Stephen Avenue enjoying the sights and sounds of the New Year's Eve festivities. They were bundled up to protect themselves from the winter's bite as they made their way around the Olympic Plaza. Cara found an ice sculpture with a built-in ice slide that she immediately, like a child, joyfully slid down. The city's core skating rink was filled with enthusiastic skaters circling the sixty-foot Christmas tree lit in all its glory. She and Angel laughed and took selfies to capture the evening's special moments. Needing to warm their fingers and toes, they entered JJ's Irish Pub to enjoy a hot chocolate topped with whipped cream before heading to their hotel room to watch the fireworks blast into the night sky off the top of the Calgary Tower.

Snuggling under the blankets, watching the fireworks light up the dark sky outside the large window of their hotel room, Angel gently placed her hand on Cara's cheek bringing them face to face. "Nights like this are so special, Cara. Being able to have you by my side not only for the evening but for the whole night gets me thinking about how wonderful it would be to live together and get to do this all the time."

"I know what you mean, Angel. I love falling asleep with you beside me and then having you there when I wake up in the morning."

"Maybe one day we could find a condo for the two of us downtown. Maybe something close to where I work now, so I could even walk."

"Downtown would be an amazing place to live together. I would love that, Angel."

Cracks and pops brought their attention back to the fireworks that had their room changing colours with each new explosion. As the last firework burst causing the sky to glow one final time, the two of them fell into their rhythm before falling asleep in the heat of each other's embrace.

CHAPTER 35

She Runs Again

Four days into the new year, Cara got a call from Jay asking if the kids could spend the night with him since they were still on Christmas break. Excited, she called Angel as soon as she had hung up with Jay.

"Hey, Angel. The kids aren't going to be with me tonight, so I was thinking, maybe you might want to come to my place and "play in the park," their new code words for a little intimate fun.

"I'm so sorry, Cara, but I already made plans to meet Justin for dinner tonight."

"No worries at all. Have a fun night with your son, and please say hi to him for me."

The next day, Cara asked Angel if she would like to join her for dinner, but Angel reminded her it was her running night.

"Oh, that's right, I forgot it was Wednesday. Isn't it too cold out today?"

"It's being held tonight in the field house."

"Ahh, that makes sense! Would tomorrow night be better for dinner, then?"

"That would work perfectly! I'll come to your place right after work, and that way I will still have time later in the evening to spend with my kids."

"That sounds great."

"Let's meet around five. Can't wait to see you."

⁂

I'll tell her I need to clean my place so I don't have to do it on the weekend, or maybe my stomach doesn't feel too good. Giving Cara a glimmer of hope is always easier than telling her the truth that I'd rather just put on my sweats and lounge on the couch for the rest of the night. Why shouldn't I? I worked hard all week and home time should be my time to do what I want. I'm sure Cara's going to tell me how much she was looking forward to being with me and that it sucks when I cancel on her, blah blah blah, whatever. This is my life. I'm going to do what feels good to me.

⁂

Cara woke the next morning to a text from Angel: *Sorry, but I need to cancel our dinner plans for this evening. I'm not feeling well. I think I'm coming down with the flu.*

Cara wrote back: *Oh my goodness, that's not good. I hope you're feeling better soon. If you need anything, call me.* ☺

Friday morning, Cara sent Angel a text: *Hope you're feeling better today?*

Angel replied: *Morning, thanks. Still not feeling 100%. You're up early.*

Cara wrote: *I went to bed so early last night that I woke up at around six this morning. Just so you know, I'm going to head to the Roughnecks game tonight with the kids.*

Angel answered, *That'll be fun. I've been invited to go to The Locked Room for a birthday party for one of the ladies at work, so I'm going out tonight.*

Cara was caught off guard. Angel wasn't feeling well, but still, she was going out.

Angel went on: *So that you know, Cara, I'm going to take the girls shopping during the day tomorrow and catch a movie at night.*

Cara replied, *That'll be nice for you to spend some special time with them.*

Angel wrote, *Do you have time to talk on the phone, Cara?*

Cara answered, *Of course.* ☺

Angel called right away. "Cara, it's too much pressure for me when you ask me to do things, and I have to turn you down. I don't think I can do this anymore."

"What?"

"I need some time to think about us. Let's talk more later."

The conversation ended as quickly as it had begun. Cara had no idea Angel had been feeling pressured by her. *How was wanting to spend time with your partner a bad thing? Wasn't it good if your partner wanted to spend time with you? Why did Angel not take the time to discuss how she was feeling? She just dropped a bomb and then walked away. What did needing time for herself mean? Was she going to end the relationship…again? Angel's reactions are becoming more and more erratic.*

Cara looked at the texts she had sent Angel. She had asked Angel out a couple of times but to her, it didn't seem like she had asked too much. When Cara returned home from the lacrosse game that night, she called Angel. "Do you have a moment to talk, Angel?"

"Yes, I do."

Cara took in a deep breath. "Angel, our relationship is very important to me, and I want you to know I am committed to us and our future together. From your call this morning, you are clearly struggling with something. I want to give you the time to figure things out, but I don't want that to mean you and I will not be together. I want to be there for you, but if you need time to be completely alone, I will respect that too. I'm hoping you will see that we are worth it and that you want to be with me. When you're ready, let's sit down and discuss everything as a couple. We need to stop having these in-and-out moments and instead focus on being committed to one another, just like we talked about last week. We will certainly face issues in the future, but if we talk to each other when those times arise, we can get through them together. I'm trying hard to give you what you need, Angel. Please don't give up on us so easily."

"I'm going to sleep on this, Cara, and talk to you in the morning."

The next morning, with Cara still lying in bed, eyes dry from barely closing all night, Angel called.

"Hi, Cara. I think taking a break at this time would be best for me. I want to meet with a psychologist to figure out why I've been feeling this way."

Cara didn't think her heart could sink any deeper in her chest. "I was hoping for a different reply but I think it's great you want to see a psychologist."

"Be honest with me, Cara. Do you think we should be together?"

Why would Angel ask her this? Had Angel not heard what she said last night and so many times before? "Angel, as I said yesterday, I am always committed to us and being together. I love you deeply, and I want to be with you. The only thing that makes me question us is when you arbitrarily decide you can't do us anymore. This has happened a few times now and it's extremely hurtful and hard on me."

"That's just what I needed to hear. The feeling in my stomach is now gone. I'm good with not being in a relationship with you. I'm going to focus on me now and what I need."

Cara sat there, phone in hand and no one on the other end, thinking, *What the heck just happened?*

CHAPTER 36

Lila and Sophie

~~~

"Cara, I'm glad you came to my place for lunch," Lila said. "I'm so sorry you keep going through this with Angel. Are you okay?"

"Thanks, Lila. I feel completely crushed. I try to give Angel what she needs, but it never seems to be enough."

"Cara, your partner is supposed to enrich your life, not drain it. Staying in it when it's hurting you is not love."

"Fuck, Cara," Sophie said. "Now that you've filled me in, too, I'm sorry Angel's been putting you through all this shit, but seriously, she sounds so fucking toxic for you."

"I don't know how to explain it, guys. I know I don't deserve what she's doing, and it isn't right, but I suck it up every time because the thought of not being with her feels worse. Every time she wants me back, I take her back!"

"I get how you enjoy her company when things are going good, Cara, but her Dr. Jekyll and Mr. Hyde personality with you borders on fucking crazy."

"She told me she's going to start seeing a psychologist…maybe that might help her be a better partner, and then maybe she'll be like she used to be when we first started dating. She was so loving and caring toward me then."

"That's if she even goes, Cara. Lila looked at her with such sad eyes. She's always telling you she'll do things but she never follows through."

"If I'm being honest Cara, hopefully, this time she just stays away. But knowing what I know now, I wouldn't fucking count on it!"

CHAPTER 37

Let's Talk

The March morning was crisp, and Cara could see a thin line of ice at the bottom of her office windows. The view from where she sat was a winter wonderland. She was trying desperately to get caught up on her business month ends for January and now February, but she didn't seem to have the energy or the drive to do anything lately.

When a ding came from her phone and she looked down, Cara gasped at the sight of Angel's name. She even did a double take, raising the phone closer to confirm she hadn't imagined it.

Hi Cara, I hope you're having a great week. Liz told me yesterday that she asked you to go with her to get her boob job surgery done in Costa Rica. Since Dan couldn't get the time off from work and you know the area well, that is kind of you; it would be scary for her to do it alone.

After reading the text three times, Cara still couldn't believe Angel had texted her. Just like the first time she had broken up with Cara, here she was again, sending her a text over a month later as if nothing had ever happened between them.

The need to respond was always strong when it came to Angel, but Cara didn't want to share what was happening in her life, so instead she just texted, *Pura Vida* along with some summertime emojis.

Within minutes, Angel replied: *Lol ☺ jealous!!! Are you doing okay?*

Cara waited over three hours to reply. The breakup had not been easy on her. She'd had good and bad days since Angel had slammed the door shut on their relationship…again. Cara wasn't going to share what she had been through, so she decided to answer with what she had just finished doing: *I was doing great until I finished my spin class. I feel like puking now!*

Angel replied, *That's awesome you're spinning! I hate spin, lol ☺ I just got back from doing my first indoor 10k!!! On my way to a 15k race at the end of April.*

Cara waited till the next morning to write, *Good for you!*

Angel replied instantly. *Cara, I'm still hurt by how everything ended when I was struggling to get over what happened at Christmas. I know you didn't want to break up, but I miss my best friend.*

Of course, Angel missed her. Angel had no other friends she could rely on like Cara. *I thought we were good after New Year's, Angel. You blindsided me when you called me days later and changed your story from "We're going to be together forever" to "I don't think I can do this anymore."*

I want to get back together, Cara. What do we do to move forward?

Did you see a psychologist like you said you would?

No; I decided I didn't want to work on things to be better for someone else. I want to work together with you so we can be together. Can we please meet and talk face-to-face?

I don't know, Angel. I'm tired of this merry-go-round you keep putting me on.

Just meet with me, Cara, and let's talk through everything. I'm free after work today.

I have too much paperwork to get caught up on tonight. Maybe tomorrow evening.

Perfect. Come to my place any time after six.

It was already dark at 5:40, as Cara drove the slippery country back roads inching her way to Angel's house in town. Her mind had been on play and rewind all day trying to get the wording right of what she wanted to say. If she and Angel were going to try again, she was determined to do things right this time. She wasn't going to jump back into a relationship with her without sitting down, communicating her needs, and hearing what Angel needed from her so that maybe this time they would have a fighting chance.

Walking up to the door, Cara was thankful for the porch lights being on. Angel hadn't shovelled her driveway or entry steps, so being able to see the treacherous walk made it a little less dangerous. She still had the key to Angel's place, but she didn't dare use it. As she reached to ring the doorbell, the dogs started barking hysterically and Angel opened the door.

"Hi, Cara. It's so nice to see you." Pushing the dogs out of Cara's way with her foot so she could come inside out of the cold.

Hanging her jacket on one of the four wall hooks, Cara removed her boots receiving a hug from Angel as soon as she stood up.

"Can I get you a tea? The kettle's all boiled."

"That sounds good. Thank you."

"Just grab a seat in the living room, Cara. I'll be right back."

As soon as both dogs jumped on the couch, tails wagging a mile a minute, Cara grabbed a spot on the single leather chair.

When Angel came back with the tea and got settled on the couch with the dogs, Cara started things off. "Angel, you say you want to get back together, but every time we do, you point out things I'm doing wrong that make you want to leave. What do you need from me to make things better for you?"

Angel took a sip of her steaming tea before saying, "I feel, that when something is bothering you, you shut down and say everything is fine instead of talking about it. I would like you to share how you feel so it doesn't build up and become something bigger than it needs to be."

What Angel was saying was true. Cara was well aware she did this, all because she never knew how Angel was going to react if she shared her actual thoughts. She wasn't about to say that now, in fear of Angel's classic comment "You're always 'justifying' Cara, instead of just listening to what I'm saying." Instead, Cara sat there sipping on her tea.

"I also feel you don't share all the details going on in your life. I know you don't ever lie to me, but you don't always tell me the full story. I want you to feel comfortable sharing everything with me, not just parts of it."

Watching Angel lean back onto the couch, Cara placed her teacup on the end table and replied to Angel's comments. "Thank you for letting me know how you feel. I hear you and I am willing to work on those things."

Angel jumped back in. "The hardest thing for me, Cara, is the pressure I feel from you always wanting to spend time with me. I work Monday to Friday, which is much different from your schedule." Cara didn't appreciate that comment. Sure, she didn't work a 9 to 5 in an office like Angel, but she worked her ass off running her own business. "I don't always have the time or the energy to go out as often as you would like. It causes me pressure when I have to say no to you."

"Angel, I'm glad you brought this up because time together is a recurring issue for us that has caused us problems from the beginning. I want to share with you, that when I get to spend time with you, it makes me feel like I am a priority in your life. It makes me feel secure in what we are building together and most importantly, it lets me know I can count on you. But know that when I ask you to go out, I realize you won't always be able to go out with me, so you don't have to feel pressured. I ask you because you are the first person I think of when I come up with things to do. I ask you because you are the person I want to share those experiences with, but I never expect that you are going to say yes every time I ask and that's okay. What I would appreciate, though, is when you can't join me, and I still go out with friends, that you're happy for me. It doesn't feel good when I second guess my choices because you don't approve of them. Going out with my friends makes me happy and it would be great if you could be happy for me too."

"I know I need to work on that, Cara because it's unfair to you when I do it. If I'm being totally honest, sometimes I'm just jealous."

"You have nothing to be jealous about, Angel; you're always my number one."

"Thank you for telling me that, Cara. Look, I want us to be together, and I'm willing to put in the effort this time to make it work."

Cara hoped this open conversation would do the trick, setting them on the right path this time. But due to Angel's track record, Cara decided she would keep their reuniting to herself, just so she wouldn't feel foolish if Angel went back on her words.

CHAPTER 38

Dr. Kendra

Not the snow whipping against Cara's living room window, nor the minus 28-degree temperatures outside were going to dampen her spirits. It was a new day and after her conversation the night prior with Angel, followed by the most peaceful of sleep, Cara woke up knowing exactly what she was going to do to make things work this time.

Cara wanted a healthy relationship and decided the way for her to give Angel what she needed was to get some help from a psychologist. To share her feelings and thoughts openly with someone she didn't know would not be easy for her, but she wanted so badly to have Angel in her life that she was willing to pull up her big girl panties and do whatever it took to make things work.

Due to how busy Dr. Kendra's schedule was, the earliest appointment Cara could get was three weeks away. Excited to share the news with Angel, she texted her. *I want you to know how serious I am about what you shared with me yesterday. Today,*

I booked an appointment with a psychologist to help me make the changes you want me to make.

That's fantastic, Cara! It's great knowing you're willing to do this for me.

Dr. Kendra's office put Cara at instant ease. Two of the walls were floor-to-ceiling bookshelves painted in bright white and filled with technical and easy-reading books. *Had Dr. Kendra read them all? If she had, that's impressive! Should I lay on the dark blue velvet couch while waiting for her or were the two orange chairs in the corner the place we'd talk?* The colourful abstract artwork displayed on the other two walls intrigued Cara; she wondered if they were Rorschach tests in disguise. She had only been there about three minutes when a voluptuous lady wearing a colourful scarf and a fitted dark blue pantsuit came sauntering through a second door opposite from where Cara had entered, holding her hand out and boasting a huge smile.

"Hello, Cara, I'm Dr. Kendra. It's a pleasure to meet you."

"Hi, Dr. Kendra. It's nice to meet you too."

"Shall we sit over here?" Dr. Kendra pointed at the orange chairs.

No lying down today. Cara thought.

"Tell me, Cara, why did you want to meet with me?" Fidgeting a little in her chair as sweat trickled down the base of her neck, hoping Dr. Kendra didn't notice her discomfort, Cara looked past her to one of the pictures and said, "My partner, Angel, told me I need to change some things I've been doing to improve our relationship. I honestly don't feel I can make these changes on my own, so I'm hoping with some guidance from you, I can correct those things."

"Are you not a good partner to her?"

"Quite the opposite. I'd do anything for her; that's why I'm here."

"I see this all the time, Cara, people coming to see me because someone wants them to change. A partner shouldn't ask you to change, but rather both partners should look into themselves to see what they can work on as individuals to better themselves, which, in turn, will help improve their relationship."

"I guess that makes sense."

"Cara, would you be okay sharing a little about your childhood, your relationship with your family, and anything that might be important for me to know to better understand who you are? Things become much clearer when we understand how our past has affected us as adults."

Cara would have rather talked about anything than her past childhood experiences. She had worked hard on keeping that stuff buried deep, but if Dr. Kendra thought it was important to discuss her past to make things better for her and Angel's relationship, she was determined to be one hundred percent open with her.

At the end of the appointment, Dr. Kendra said, "Cara, thank you for being vulnerable and sharing as much as you did. I know the main reason you came is for your relationship, but your back story tells me so much about who you are and how you view things, which in turn helps me to help you. I think the book *Hold Me Tight* by Sue Johnson will be an excellent start for your relationship and I think it would be very beneficial if we met again next week to delve a little deeper into some of your childhood trauma."

Cara thanked Dr. Kendra and then went directly to the bookstore. She texted Angel before pulling out of her parking spot: *The meeting was amazing, Angel...I found it eye-opening, and I was surprised it wasn't as hard as I thought it would be to open up and share. She gave me the name of a book she thought I should read, and I already have another appointment set up for next week.*

Angel replied instantly, *That's awesome, Cara! I'm glad it went well!*

I'm going to go grab the book and then head home to start reading. Would you be available tomorrow after work to meet up, so I can share things that were discussed in the meeting today?

Yes, that sounds great.

Cara texted, *Maybe you could grab the book on your way home from work too, so we could work through it together.*

When they met the following evening at the King Henry, Angel immediately pulled out the book as she sat down. "I want you to know I'm serious about working on us too."

"I'm so happy to hear that, Angel. Thanks for picking up a copy for yourself."

"So, tell me about what you've read so far."

"The book discusses emotional dependency and the need to feel safe and secure in a relationship. When there's a disconnect and you don't feel safe and secure, heavy conversations resort to couples blaming the other to try and prove they are right."

"That does sound like us, Cara."

"You're right about that."

"What, a mischievous look on Angel's face appeared.

Giggling, "Yes, you are right Angel." Knowing how Angel loved to hear Cara say she was right and then say 'what' just so she could hear Cara say you're right again. "The book explains how each person reacts when blaming arguments happen. One person tries to get an emotional reaction out of their partner, and the other partner usually shuts down. I think this book can help us, Angel."

Angel raised her shoulders, a look of disbelief on her face, "Maybe," before saying, "This past week has kind of sucked for me, Cara, because I haven't spent time with you."

"Why didn't you just call and ask me to hang out?"

"I wasn't sure if it was okay to call you or if I should text because I wasn't sure what to do. I'm so scared I will hurt you, or even worse, be hurt."

Cara reached across the table and held Angel's hands. "Hopefully, through reading this book, we can figure out ways to effectively communicate and work through how we've handled things in the past, so we can do things differently this time."

Angel looked at Cara. "I think we just need to do things more slowly so we don't fall back into repeating patterns."

"That sounds good to me. Let's keep meeting like this, talking about things in the book and just taking baby steps."

Angel's frown made Cara think that maybe her comment wasn't what Angel wanted. "How would you like us to proceed, Angel?"

"I think it's a good idea to keep reading the book and doing some of the work together, but I also want us to continue our relationship being us and just enjoy being together and not making it all about the book."

Cara felt a bit perplexed. 'Just being us' had not worked in the past, and 'Just being us' would not change the problematic patterns that kept repeating. While Cara tried to make sense of what Angel had just said, Angel changed the subject to her daughter.

"I want to let you know, Cara that Jayden's been struggling lately and she'll be staying home more often than going to her dad's on our weekends. She needs to be my number-one priority, but don't worry; I'll still make time for you. Let's see a movie this Saturday afternoon and then have some playtime together at your place. Intimate time is important and will help us stay connected."

Cara felt bad for Angel that her daughter was struggling. She knew how hard it was as a parent whenever your child wasn't doing well. All you want is to take that pain away from them. Hearing Angel say she still wanted to see Cara and also incorporate some playtime this weekend, was music to Cara's ears. "I'd like to tell you something too, Angel that's not very easy for me to talk about."

Looking at Cara intently, "Sure, what is it?"

When I was talking to Dr. Kendra, she asked if I would share some of my past experiences, so she could better understand me. I told her something that hardly anyone knows. I've tried to forget it due to how horrible it was to go through, but after sharing it with her, I felt better. Kind of like a weight lifted from letting go of the secret."

"You can share anything with me, Cara."

"I want to be open with you and even though it's hard to talk about, Dr Kendra said it's important to share my past with you, for you to better understand me." Pausing and taking a moment to compose herself, Cara opened up saying, "When I was just a little kid, my oldest brother sexually molested me."

"Cara, my estranged brother told my family a similar story, except he said his daughter told him it was one of my uncles that did something to her. My brother has always been kind of out there, so I don't know if I believe him. I like that Uncle. I don't think he would have done such a thing."

Cara sat in shock, her eyes showing her dismay. "Kids don't make that stuff up, Angel. They should always be believed when they tell someone. *Why hadn't she acknowledged what I shared with her.* I'm really surprised none of you believed her."

"If you only knew my brother, Cara, you would understand why."

Cara didn't feel the same way, sharing her secret with Angel, as she had with Dr. Kendra.

CHAPTER 39

Will Things Ever Change

❦

Angel picked Cara up at two thirty to head to the movie. "How's the reading going, Cara?"

"I can barely put it down, I'm getting so much out of it. What do you think of the book?"

Angel pursed her lips. "I've read a lot of it and thought it was pretty good, but I also thought you need to put into practice what it says for it to do any good."

Cara thought that was a weird comment. Wasn't that why they were reading it? To put into practice what they were learning?

After the movie, when they returned to Cara's place, she noticed Angel had brought her book in and placed it on the table. They hadn't discussed doing anything with the book today, but Cara was up for it if Angel wanted to.

"It's so weird, Cara; even though Jayden knows where I am, she's still texting me asking when I'll be home."

"Do you need to go now, Angel?"

"Not before some playtime."

Running toward the bedroom, Cara flung her clothes off along the way. Turning momentarily toward Angel with a mischievous smile before jumping backwards spread eagle onto the bed. Their sexual connection was undeniable. They knew each other's bodies and what each other liked. It wasn't just the lovemaking that made it so special, it was also the intimate cuddling and caressing afterward, enjoying the beautiful moment they had just shared.

Angel looked at Cara. "How silly we've been. We waste so much time not being together."

"Well, that's all going to change because we're figuring things out, Angel! What a perfect end to a great day. Thank you for spending time with me."

The next morning, Cara sent Angel an inspirational quote from Eric Thomas that seemed fitting for what they had been going through: *Don't think about what can happen in a month. Don't think about what can happen in a year. Just focus on the twenty-four hours before you and do what you can to get closer to where you want to be.* Below it, Cara wrote, *Good morning, beautiful!*

Angel replied immediately, *Hi, can I call you? I'm not doing good.*

Absolutely! Cara was going to put into practice everything she had been reading, including the tips Dr. Kendra had told her. Whatever Angel had to say, she would not take it personally. She would listen and reply compassionately, so Angel would know she was hearing her and was there for her.

"I woke up around three thirty and was feeling scared. I was waiting for you to text me, so I could call you."

"Let me know why you are feeling this way, Angel."

"Everything is moving too fast. I don't want to get hurt and I don't want to hurt you." Angel didn't say anything else, so Cara said, "I'm so glad you're sharing how you feel, Angel. This is exactly what we need to do when we struggle with our thoughts… talk to each other and figure it out together. We need to slow down if you're scared about us moving too fast. I have no problem with taking baby steps forward."

"I'm so happy you understand, Cara."

Cara was beyond proud of herself for handling the situation completely differently from how she might have handled it in the past. She did not take what Angel was saying as a personal attack; instead, she wanted to give Angel the reassurance she needed by letting her know she understood, that she could be there for her, and that everything would be okay. "Is there anything else you want to talk about, Angel?"

"Nope, I'm all good. That was everything. Thanks, Cara, for letting me share how I felt and for being so receptive."

Later that day, Cara sent a text to Angel: *Hi, just checking in to ensure you're doing okay.*

Angel replied, *I'm doing good. Talking to you this morning helped. I got everything done that I wanted to do today, and now I'm going for a nap. Are you okay?*

Cara wrote, *I'm doing great. I'm glad talking earlier helped you. I hope you have a great nap.*

The next morning, as Cara was working in her office, a text came through from Angel: *Cara, I'm so sorry to do this to you. For once, I need to listen to what my body is telling me. This no longer feels right to me. There have been too many breakups and too much pain. I will always love you and hope you find the happiness and joy you deserve.*

Cara shouldn't have been shocked, but she was. Even though this was how Angel had handled their relationship so many times before, Cara still sat in dead silence, wondering to herself, *WTF!!!*

Why did Angel continually want her back, only to crush her heart and spirit time after time? Why did Cara believe Angel when she said she would try harder and wanted to work on saving their relationship, when all Angel ever did was talk a big talk and then run? Angel's words were like a puff of smoke; looks impressive at first but dissipates quickly. Did anything from Angel's lips ever hold an ounce of truth? Here Cara was, trying to fix what Angel said was broken within Cara, but Angel did nothing and then gave up.

Cara took some time to get her head in a good place before replying. *Angel, this is scary for both of us because neither of us wants to hurt the other. Even though we are just starting to work on ourselves, these early conversations and reading the book have been positive steps in the right direction. I want to show you I can be here for you, especially when you are struggling. I know from what you've told me these last couple of weeks that you want us to be together, but you're scared. Just keep taking small steps forward because I'm not going anywhere. Let's meet again tonight to talk out these feelings you are experiencing. I love you.*

Angel wrote back, *You have to let go, Cara. I cannot do this anymore. It is physically and mentally hurting me. Please do not push this.*

CHAPTER 40

Change Is Growth

~~~

Running her index finger along the spine of a very thick Psychology book, Cara turned from the white shelving unit to see the woman who had guided her out of a very dark place. "Seeing you weekly for the last six months has opened my eyes to so many things, Dr. K."

"You've been doing the work, Cara and have come leaps and bounds from when we first met."

Walking past the row upon row of books, Cara asked, "I've always wondered…have you read all these books?"

Smiling that big smile Cara was met with at the beginning of each session, Dr Kendra said, "Most of them I have."

"Wow, that's impressive!" Dr. Kendra's office had always been a safe space for Cara. Cara had heard that some people switch up their psychologists until they find a good match, but for Cara, Dr.

Kendra fit like a glove from the get-go. "I too, feel I have changed Dr. K."

"Do you care to expand?"

As Cara made her way around the room, hands in her front pockets, she noted the rich colour of the palm tree soil; last week it looked like the salt flats of Utah. "I was not in a good head space back in May. I was struggling trying to make sense of everything. I was so confused by it all and deeply hurt by the way Angel had ended us. What saved me was you telling me to write about my experiences. Writing was brutally cathartic for me and it helped me not only begin to process my childhood experience and how it impacted me in adulthood but writing about my relationship with Angel made me see what gradually happened to me over time."

"Tell me more, Cara."

Taking a seat across from Dr. Kendra, Cara inhaled deeply and then exhaled saying, "I can sum it up in five words: what I allow will continue."

"Yes, Cara! It's all about boundaries. Whether it is a friend, family member, or partner, we must have boundaries."

"I always felt I had healthy boundaries with my children, friends, and even my ex-husband, but somehow my boundaries went out the window when I got into a relationship with Angel."

"That's because of who she is, Cara. From everything you've shared with me in our sessions, Angel presents classic covert narcissist traits and very likely suffers from narcissistic personality disorder."

Cara smacked the palm of her hand to her forehead. "If only I had listened to Lila when she first told me about that Dr. Phil episode on narcissism."

"We all learn our lessons at different times, Cara. You told me you were in love with Angel and love can blind us to the real character of a person when we don't take the time to get to know who they truly are before jumping in head over heels."

"I see that now. I fell hard for Angel, and I lost myself in the process."

"Narcissistic people are masters at manipulating and controlling their surroundings. When they do this repeatedly, they trauma bond their partners. That's one of the reasons you didn't have healthy boundaries with her; you didn't even realize the trauma was building because of how gradually it happens. The breakup and back together, repeat, repeat, repeat, form the trauma bond so that it becomes an addiction, like a drug you can't get enough of."

Cara needed a few minutes to compose herself. Rising from her seat she walked over to the velvet couch and laid down, closing her eyes briefly to hold back the tears. She had spent months processing and coming to terms with the toxic relationship she had allowed into her life but even so, it never got easier hearing the person she believed was the love of her life, the person she thought she would spend the rest of her life with, was the same person that had caused her so much internal damage. Cara wondered if Angel realized the pain and hurt she had caused and if she did, did she even care? Cara was proud of herself for the personal growth she had made but knew more time was still needed to heal. "I just wanted her to love me Dr. K., and be there for me like I was for her. She was so loving to me initially, but as you know, the longer we were together it all changed."

"That's the thing with narcissists, Cara. At first, they will give you everything you have told them you need. They create a façade to lure you in, making you think you have met your soulmate because they mirror what they know you are looking for. They have honed the skill of impressing their sources, but eventually, the narcissist's needs will always come first. They may show you love and act lovingly, but it tends to be conditional because they truly don't know how to love in a normal, healthy way. Relationships tend to be transactional for people with NPD. Unless they have something to gain from you, they lose interest."

Spreading the palms of her hands out against the softness of the velvet couch, little goose bumps popped from Cara's skin. Not sure if she wanted to hear the answer to the next question, she blurted it out anyway. "Do you think she ever actually loved me?"

"From all you've shared, Cara, I believe Angel loved you in the only way she knew how. She kept enticing you back because she saw beautiful, positive qualities in you that she wanted for herself. I'm sure she has her own deep emotional wounds, most likely caused during her childhood, but that's not an excuse for her damaging behaviour toward you."

Looking over at Dr. Kendra, Cara propped herself up on her elbows. "Being with Angel was such an emotional rollercoaster ride for me."

"We learn from all our experiences, Cara. Because of what you've been through, you'll now notice red flags in future relationships, allowing you to make better decisions."

"I have you to thank for that, Dr. K."

"From all our sessions, what do you think is the most important thing you've learned?"

Cara reflected biting her lower lip and fiddling with the bottom of her sweater. "I believe I learned the importance behind talking about and dealing with what happened to me when I was seven."

"Can you expand on that?"

Sitting up and facing Dr. Kendra, Cara did her best to explain. "When the abuse first started, I didn't tell anyone because I felt ashamed like it was my fault somehow for why someone who was supposed to love me was taking advantage of me. Even though I was young I knew what Damien was doing was wrong, but when I told him I didn't like it and I wanted him to stop, he continued. He controlled me and I was being taught that my voice didn't matter. The note I wrote to my mom when I was nine years old is what finally made the abuse stop. Maybe that's one of the reasons

I write, Dr. K., because it's the only way I believe people will hear what I have to say."

"I'm sure that holds some truth, Cara."

"After it was all over, the abuse was never spoken about again and I was told not to tell anyone, leaving me no outlet to process what I'd been through. Instead, I came up with a coping mechanism to stop reliving the abuse. I taught myself to bury and block the things in life that could make me feel pain or hurt to stay in control of my thoughts and emotions. If I didn't allow myself to feel, I was the one in control."

"You were taking back your control, Cara."

"I know it helped me at the time, Dr. K., but you taught me that because I never dealt with the trauma, it followed me into adulthood."

"Yes, Cara. If we don't work through childhood trauma, it has a way of reeling its ugly head somewhere down the road. I'm so glad that you understand that now."

"I think subconsciously as an adult, I didn't believe I deserved any better when it came to someone loving me. I believed I needed to settle for whatever 'love' I could get, and that I should do whatever it took to hold on to that 'love', even at my own expense. I didn't understand my worth, Dr. K., and I wasn't giving myself any credit for how much I bring to a relationship."

"You formed an extremely unhealthy attachment to Angel, always rationalizing and defending her abusive actions, in hopes that her behaviour would change."

"I see all that now. I wish I would have seen it earlier."

"You're not the first to have this happen to them, Cara, and you certainly won't be the last."

"Am I crazy to still feel love for her?"

"The heart is not so easily wiped clean, Cara. I believe you truly did love her. But what you experienced in your relationship with Angel was not love. Trauma bonds resemble love, but trauma bond relationships are driven by fear, not love. You constantly feared losing her due to your innate fear of being alone. That is the main reason why you allowed the abuse to continue."

"What if she ever wants me back again?"

"That is a choice you will have to make. At least now, you have the tools to create a healthy relationship and know how to set healthy boundaries for yourself."

"Dr. K., I can't thank you enough for everything you've done for me."

CHAPTER 41

Moving to the City

❧

THE WARM DAYS of summer were coming to an end. Cara felt reenergized as she walked through the streets of downtown Calgary looking for a new place to live. Life was changing for her. Cody was going into his last year of high school, and Dani was moving into her own place close to the university she would be attending in the fall. Moving would keep Cara close enough to her daughter if she needed her momma, but far enough away to let Dani spread her wings.

Cara loved the city for its restaurants, bars, and music venues. It didn't take much convincing to get Cody on board; once he saw the spectacular sub-penthouse view and learned he would get the main suite with a private bathroom, he was all for the move.

When the rental agreement had been signed, Cara texted all her friends to let them know her exciting news.

Congratulations and can't wait to help you move in, came from Lila. *So excited for you, and can't wait to party up that high,* came from Sophie. Other kind notes like *looking forward to seeing your new place,* and *that's just amazing, Cara, so happy for you,* all started streaming in.

Even though Cara hadn't seen Angel for ages, she still received texts from her now and then updating Cara on her mom's condition or something that had happened to her at work. Just the week prior, Cara had received a text that said, *Here's my new cell number; I would hate to have you think I don't care if you ever tried to contact me and didn't have the correct number.*

There was no reason for Cara to let Angel know she was moving, but still, Cara wanted her to know. It wasn't so Angel would have her address; it was more to let her know she was moving forward with her life and doing well.

After debating for over an hour whether to send the text or not, Cara texted, *Hey, Angel just wanted to share that I'm moving downtown! Super excited!!!*

To Cara's surprise, an instant reply came back: *Oh, well, that's interesting. I've been looking at places to move downtown too.*

Angel worked downtown, so it made sense that she should live there, but Cara knew Angel's percentage of follow-through was extremely low, so the likelihood of that happening was slim. Cara didn't receive a *Congratulations* or *I'm so excited for you,* from Angel. She knew a positive reaction from Angel was always highly dependent on three things: Angel's mood, whether it benefitted Angel, and the number of alcoholic beverages Angel had consumed.

Cara recalled a time she had purchased an abstract painting of a half-naked woman from a young local artist. Cara had thought it was a beautiful piece, but when she showed it to Angel, all she got was, "Hmm, that's different," because Angel had been in a pissy mood that day. Weeks later, when they had made love and Angel saw the painting hanging on Cara's bedroom wall, she told Cara, "That is such a beautiful painting."

Another time, Cara shared with Angel a tattoo design she was planning on getting. It was an old-style piece of luggage with a little ladybug on it to represent having the travel bug. Due to the old luggage piece being Angel's idea of a tattoo she wanted to get one day, Angel made it very clear to Cara that she did not want her to get the same tattoo. But only months later, when Angel was happy and all lovey-dovey with Cara, she said, "We should go get matching tattoos."

Adding too much alcohol into the equation only heightened Angel's reactions to Cara. Her demeanour could change from the most loving girlfriend to deep-seated anger toward Cara. One of those times forever burned in Cara's mind was after a company Christmas function of Angel's. Even though they had a fantastic time during the party, everything changed on the ride home. Since it was Angel's work party, Cara had offered to be the designated driver that night, having a few drinks early on and then stopping. Angel, of course, drank all evening. Since they both had their kids at home that night, no plans had been made to sleep at either one of their places, but just before they arrived at Angel's house, Angel decided she wanted Cara to stay over. She made it clear to Cara that they wouldn't be having sex because her kids were home, but she wanted Cara there so she had someone to snuggle with. Cara remembered treading lightly, letting Angel know she would've loved to, but her kids were expecting her home that night. Her answer was all it took for Angel's mood to do a one-eighty. When they reached Angel's driveway and Cara put the car in park so she could kiss Angel goodnight, Angel jumped out of the vehicle before Cara could even hug her goodbye. When she saw Angel struggling to gather the Christmas gifts and centrepiece from the car's back seat, Cara asked if she could help. Angel looked at Cara with googly eyes, saying, "No, I got it," slamming the door so hard she almost fell over. Cara waited like she always did when dropping Angel off to ensure she got in safely. As Angel fumbled with her keys to open her front door, Cara opened the car window and once again asked if she could help. At that moment, Angel unlocked her door, turned around, and started yelling. "Fuck you, Cara. Fuck you."

Knowing Angel was drunker than a skunk, she just closed her window and drove away. Cara grimaced at that memory, instantly feeling the same gut-wrenching hurt at the thought of those harsh demeaning words coming from the person she had loved. The following day, upon waking, Cara received a text from Angel apologizing profusely for how she had acted, even sharing that she had even talked poorly to Jayden that night and felt so ashamed for how she had treated them both. Angel shared that Jayden even said, "Mom, why are you screaming like that at Cara? It's not her fault you're drunk."

With all the crazy ways Angel had acted in the past, Cara shouldn't have expected her great news to elicit something positive from Angel because she now knew if it didn't benefit Angel, Angel wouldn't care.

While Cara was on her laptop paying her rent online for only the second time, her cell phone rang. Looking toward her iPhone she saw that it was Angel calling. *Hmm, wonder what she wants?*

"Hi, Cara. Since it's such a gorgeous October day, I was wondering if you would like to walk with me during my lunch break."

"I was already planning a walk today, so sure, the company would be nice."

Fourth Street was lively. Cara embraced the ambiance of packed patios and happy people strolling down the streets enjoying the last of the warm weather. There wasn't a cloud in the sky, and her skin soaked in the twenty-two-degree temperature, boosting her spirits even higher. Turning onto Twenty-sixth Avenue brought them through tree-lined streets and period architecture homes where they could hear birds chirping harmoniously.

"So, what's it like living downtown? Are you glad you decided to move?" Angel asked.

"I *love* living downtown, Angel. There is so much to see and do, and I can walk everywhere." By Angel's smile, Cara could see Angel was in a good mood and seemed genuinely happy for her. "How have things been for you, Angel?"

"I've been okay, but I haven't been doing much. I go to work, and then I go home."

"Not me, I'm out all the time. I go to happy hour with friends or long walks down by the river. I've had the most amazing time since I moved downtown."

Conversation flowed for the next forty-five minutes, with many laughs along the way. As the walk wound down, Angel stopped and stood in front of Cara, taking both of Cara's hands. "Cara, my life is not the same without you. I miss you all the time. When I think about us, the positives far outweigh the negatives. There have been so many more good times than bad times."

Cara didn't say a word.

"I talked to Liz about us. I told her I treat you poorly when I am drinking. I don't know why I do it, Cara, but I need to stop."

Cara's eyes widened. She couldn't believe what Angel had shared with her sister. *Was she actually taking responsibility for something she did?*

"If I need to stop drinking as much or completely, I'm willing to do that for you, Cara. You mean so much to me, and I want you in my life."

Cara was taken aback. It was not like Angel to take responsibility for anything that went wrong when it came to the two of them. *"Had their time apart changed Angel this time?"* "Angel, I've always wanted you to be part of my life, but the mistake I've made over and over is allowing you to treat me the way you have. I'm not the same person you walked away from last time. I've worked on myself, and I need you to understand that I'll never allow you or anyone for that matter to disrespect me in the ways you have. I'm not willing to jump back into a relationship with you just because of what you are telling me today. I need to see through your actions not just your words that you're serious about what you're telling me."

"I'm willing to do whatever it takes, Cara, to have you back."

"I need to be very clear with you, Angel. If you ever treat me like you have in the past, I will walk away, and we will never be together again as friends or as partners."

CHAPTER 42

Going in the Right Direction

Cara was excited to introduce Lila to a downtown cocktail bar she had recently been to with Sophie. This Thursday was proving to be just like every other day the past three weeks with snow, snow and more snow. If December was any indication, it was going to be a long cold winter. Believer's Cocktail Lounge was a quick six blocks from Cara's building. It would be an easy walk for her, but Lila on the other hand had to drive from south Calgary through all the snow into the downtown Beltline. Cara hoped for Lila's sake the roadways from her home to 17th Ave., would be clear. Cara had reserved seats for the two of them up at the bar, where she now sat watching the bartenders create fabulous cocktails while waiting for Lila to arrive. Right on schedule, Lila walked through the doors at six sharp with sticky snow clinging to her everywhere. Cara watched as she stomped her boots in the entryway courteous not to trek too much snow into the bar.

"This place is so cool, Cara. The retro décor with the deep purple velvet seats gives off such a vibe. You sure know some great spots to grab a drink"

"I can't take credit for this one, Lila. Sophie brought me here last week. Seven-dollar two-ounce cocktails all day Monday through Thursday. It doesn't get much better!"

"You're talking my language. Those eighteen-dollar cocktail places are too rich for this girl. Oh, let's order one of those to share, watching a large fishbowl drink being delivered to the couple beside them."

With the first sips taken, Cara said, "I appreciate you coming all the way downtown. There's something I've been wanting to share with you."

"What's that?" Taking another large sip.

"I know you'll think this is crazy, or maybe you'll think I'm crazy, but I've been seeing Angel here and there for almost two months and I've decided to get back together with her."

Lila paused mid-sip, her eyes rising locking into Cara's. Letting the straw drop from her lips, "You know I'm always here to support you, Cara, no matter what. I just hope, with everything you've been through with Angel, that you've thought this through."

"I have, Lila. You know how much time I've spent with Dr. Kendra. She has taught me so much and has made me completely aware so that I won't make the same mistakes. I have also had a much different conversation with Angel when she approached me about wanting to get back together."

"What was different?"

Stirring her drink with the red and white paper straw, Cara continued. "Angel told her sister that she treats me poorly when she drinks."

"Wait, Angel took responsibility for something?"

"I know right? Hearing that from her was huge. These last couple of months, she's walked the walk, Lila, by rarely drinking when we meet up."

"That's a step in the right direction for Angel because she was not a nice person to you when she drank, but honestly, Angel wasn't all that nice to you even when she was sober."

"I made it abundantly clear, that there are no more chances if she disrespects me again. I clarified my boundaries and what would happen if she crossed them."

"I'm so proud of you for communicating that."

"Me too, Lila."

"All I want is for you to be happy and no matter what happens, I'll always be here for you, Cara." Lila pulled her in for a hug. "I'm glad you finally see what you bring to a relationship. You're an amazing partner with so much love to give. Don't ever let anyone take that away from you or make you feel less than the beautiful person you are."

"I won't ever allow that to happen again, Lila. I promise!"

The January wind was cold and blustery as Cara struggled to open the main door into the Cash Casino, where she was meeting Angel for a pre-birthday beverage to celebrate Cara turning fifty-two years young.

Cara had arrived first and grabbed a stool up at the bar. After removing her jacket and tidying up her wind-blown hair, Angel was making her way toward her. Cara loved the tingling feeling within her body whenever she saw Angel. How excited it made her feel to see Angel's dimples form quotation marks on either side of her brilliant smile when they locked eyes. Cara memorized moments like these and stored those times as photographs within her mind.

"You look absolutely beautiful, Angel."

"Ah," Angel said, her bottom lip pouting. "Thank you."

While Angel took off her coat and scarf, Cara felt elated knowing this beautiful woman in front of her was her girlfriend. When Angel sat down, Cara scooted her barstool in close. Leaning in for a hug, Angel's cherry blossom body spray ignited Cara's senses as Angel softly whispered, "Happy Birthday" into Cara's ear.

"Thank you," sneaking a kiss to Angel's neck before the hug ended.

Angel pulled out a card and a small, cube-shaped wrapped present from her purse.

"Ooh, I love presents!" Cara's heart thumped with happiness and butterflies danced in her belly after she had read the expressions of love Angel had written. "You have no idea, Angel, how your words touch me. Thank you for this beautiful card."

"It's all true. Now open your gift."

Cara removed the burgundy ribbon and the sparkly grey wrapping paper. Inside was a shiny, silver-wired ring.

"May I?" Angel asked, placing it on Cara's ring finger.

Cara held her left hand up to take in all its brilliance. Without a second thought, she placed her hand behind Angel's neck, pulling her in for a deep kiss.

"I love it, Angel."

"I'm so glad. I wasn't sure if you would like the style, but I thought it would look great on you, and it does."

"I love it. Thank you so much."

"Cara, I'm so thankful you'll always be part of my life. Let's order one drink and then make our way to Don's Dinner Theatre for the second part of your birthday gift…supper and a play."

The play was entertaining, and the buffet was tasty and filling. When it was over, they both rolled out of the venue stuffed and laughing. At their cars, Cara pulled Angel in close. "I'm so glad we finally figured out how to make things work for us."

"Me too, Cara. It helps that I'm not drinking as much."

"You've also been amazing about making time for me too, Angel. I appreciate it so much."

"I love you, Cara, and Happy Birthday."

CHAPTER 43

Costa Rica

"Hey Cara, it's March and winter doesn't seem to be giving up. How about you and I book a trip to your favourite place in the world to get away from the cold for a bit."

"Costa Rica? You want to go to Costa Rica?"

"Yes! What do you think?"

"You don't have to ask me twice. I'm in."

For Cara, travelling with Angel had always been the closest thing to perfection in their relationship. They were so in sync when on holiday. Their schedules linked up seamlessly, with waking up and going to bed, being hungry, and being ready at the same time for pool and ocean dips. They also both loved to explore together and experience whatever the place they were visiting had to offer.

When they landed in Costa Rica three and half weeks later and walked out of the airport, they were met by Juan, their private driver from the hotel holding up a sign with both their names on it. They had chosen accommodations not far from the airport as they would be jetting off early the next morning to the Caribbean side of the country. The ten-room sanctuary was like a private oasis hidden within the bustling capital city of San José. Greenery and colourful flowers were in abundance. Quickly dropping their bags in the room, they made their way to a black bistro-style table next to the pool. The air was silent. Only the soft Spanish music emanating from behind the bar could be heard. They ordered nachos with fresh Pico de Gallo and two fruity drinks. That first sip, like angels dancing on Cara's tongue.

Like the hotel's entrance, the pool too offered an atmosphere of paradise with all the lush tropical foliage. Guaria Morada, Costa Rica's national flower, lined the pool's far side, offering purple hues among the green ground covering and orchids of yellow, red, and orange. Terracotta pots filled with short and tall ferns were interspersed. Palm trees were positioned perfectly around the courtyard to offer guests much-needed shade from the day's heat. The sun was now slowly making its way to rest. The once-bright clear blue skies took on an orangey hue, readying for the night to take over and for the stars to come alive.

After enjoying their snack, Angel asked, "Do you mind if I jump into the pool for a minute to cool down?"

Sticking her toe in to see if she should join, Cara said, "The water is a little cool for me, Angel, but please go ahead, I'll just sit here and watch you." Winking at her while taking a sip of her drink.

Cara admired her girlfriend's body as she floated on her back a lime-green noodle behind her neck to help keep her afloat. Angel wore a black one-piece bathing suit sporting a crisscross fabric pattern along the front; exposing parts of Angel's skin from the centre of her breasts to just above her belly button. Cara took in all of its splendour. Her temperature rose, not sure from the heat in the air or the sensuality exuding from Angel, but when she caught Angel's eye, she smiled and said, "You look so incredibly sexy. Let's go to bed!"

The flight the next morning on an eight-seater puddle jumper was more like an adventure tour than a plane ride with views along the route being simply spectacular. Cara and Angel were in awe flying over the breathtaking jungle canopy that went on for miles and when the ocean came into view, Cara was captivated by the pristine coastline, the clear blue water, and the huge crashing waves rolling into shore. The landing was on a narrow runway parallel to the beach, so close to the water that the ocean spray could have cooled them down if the plane windows had opened.

The town of Puerto Viejo offered a variety of accommodations, but they'd booked a boutique-style hotel on the beach just outside of the main town to enjoy the peace and tranquillity. After checking in, they received a welcome cocktail topped with a colourful pink umbrella from the bartender.

"This is going to be amazing, Cara!" Angel said.

"Right!"

The Azul Inn, with only twelve rooms, was set back fifty meters from the beach, with ocean views peeking through the lush natural gardens. Cara instantly knew that her choice to book this place was the right one. The Inn looked like a treehouse, with second-floor rooms hosting large balconies facing the water. The whole building was constructed using local teak wood, including the restaurant tables and chairs, blending beautifully with the surrounding landscape. A narrow stream had been constructed alongside the dining area and filled with varying sizes of colourful fish and the cutest turtle family. A wooden walkway past the bar guided guests to the beach where individual palapas and cushioned lounge chairs sat waiting to take in the views.

Walking the dirt path from their hotel into town, Cara couldn't get over the little houses perched on stilts. "Aren't the homes in town just fabulous, Angel?"

"They sure are. They're so colourful and vibrant. I love them."

"Nobody is rushing around. Everyone seems so laid back."

"The place puts me in instant vacation mode, Cara."

"I agree. Let's grab some food at this tiny restaurant," Cara pointed to a little hut with the yummiest of smells emanating from it. White plastic chairs and tables covered in bright orange cloths sat under forty-foot palm trees with stunning views of the ocean.

Munching on calamari, fresh fish and French fries, Cara leaned back in her chair and said, "This is heaven."

"I couldn't agree with you more, Cara and that food was amazing?"

"I don't think I can eat another bite. We should hire someone to take us out to Uva Beach, the one we read about back home. It's supposed to be the best one in the area and if I remember correctly, it should only be fifteen to twenty minutes further North"

To Cara's right, a man's voice was inserted into their conversation. "No problem, mun. I take you two all oh-ver."

Cara looked over to see a man drinking from a coconut.

"You hire me. I'm a local tour guide. Here's my card."

Cara looked at Angel and shrugged. "He's got a business card. Should be okay."

Angel's body language sent out nervous vibes, but after swigging back the last of her beer, she said, "Let's do it."

The experience turned out to be like no other. Marley took them on a hike, sharing his knowledge of everything they encountered. He led them to a short rock climb up to a cliff's edge where they could see an enormous boulder shooting out of the sea two hundred feet into the air, topped with green foliage, giving it a hairlike appearance, similar to Siwash Rock off the seawall in Vancouver. Waves crashed all around it, causing an ocean spray with each hit. As they continued their hike, walking through the jungle paths, Cara's surroundings had her feeling a certain way. She reached out and placed Angel's hand in hers. It was as if the earth's energy was sharing something with her. She felt complete peace, treasuring every moment and step she took. This was the closest experience Cara had ever had of feeling connected with the universe.

"This place is magical, Angel."

CHAPTER 44

Angel Goes Backward

~~~

After being home for only two weeks, Cara was thankful that winter had not lingered into April and green grass was now popping up everywhere. It was almost eight o'clock and she was excited waiting in her office for the Zoom call to begin. A flu bug had been running rampant lately so instead of an actual party, Liz decided a Zoom call was the next best thing so she could hear all about the Costa Rica adventures they had been on. Lila wouldn't be joining them due to a personal commitment that evening, but they'd been together a couple of times already since her return home from holiday, so Lila was all caught up. Sophie would be on the call…just joining a little late.

"Hey Liz, Thanks so much for setting this all up," Cara said when she saw her face on the screen.

"My friend Sherryl dropped by tonight, so she's going to be part of our call. We're both excited to hear about the trip...over a couple glasses of wine, of course."

"Of course," Cara giggled. "Glad you could join us, Sherryl."

"I hope I'm not crashing the get-together."

"Of course not. Happy that you both are here. Wait, Angel is joining in."

"Hi, Cara. Good to see you, sis. Hey Sherryl, nice to see you too. Who else is joining tonight?"

Cara piped in, "The last two to join will be Sophie and her friend Gwen. They were at a late-afternoon function, so they'll be joining shortly."

"Not Gwen," Angel blurted. "I don't like her!"

Liz added, "I love Sophie, but Gwen, ugh, she's so loud."

Before another word could be said, both Sophie and Gwen popped onto the screen. The first words out of Gwen's mouth were, "How'd you two lovers enjoy your trip?"

Sherryl's wine sprayed from her mouth, "You two lovers?"

"Thanks for just outing us to Sherryl, Gwen," Cara said doing her best to just laugh it off.

Liz quickly changed the subject. "So tell us about the trip, ladies."

"It was amazing, Liz. Angel and I toured all over. The beaches on the Caribbean side of Costa Rica are gorgeous."

In true Gwen fashion, she jumped back in. "Hey, whoever that lady is who didn't know about Cara and Angel, I bet you have lots of questions you'd like to ask them."

The previous banter came to a stop, with surprised looks on everyone's faces except Gwen's.

"I actually do have a question," Sherryl said. "How long have the two of you been together?"

Cara was flabbergasted at Gwen's comment and froze thinking, *This is my personal life and it's nobody's business.*

Angel must have seen the look on Cara's face and jumped in saying, "We've been in a relationship for quite a while now."

"Why don't you tell her exactly how long it's been, Angel?" Gwen said with a smug look.

Gwen barely knew Cara or Angel, and here she was throwing her two cents in as if trying to stir something up. "You know what guys," Cara said, "I'm happy to answer any questions Sherryl might have, but I don't feel our Zoom call is the place where any of this needs to be discussed."

Liz was quick to redirect the conversation with another story, ending what Gwen had started.

A couple of hours passed with Sophie and Gwen being the first to leave the Zoom call.

"I swear," Cara said, "every time I have been out with Sophie and Gwen happens to be there, it's always the same. She always says something that upsets me."

"I hear you, Cara. That girl has zero social skills. Sorry, you had to meet her." Clinking Sherryl's wine glass.

"I'm glad you see it too, Liz," Cara said. "I've made a point lately to have as little interaction with Gwen as possible. If I know she'll be there when Sophie asks me out, I politely decline. I love Sophie too, but Gwen, that girl gets under my skin."

"I agree!" Liz said. "The one time I was out with all of you and Gwen showed up, she rubbed me the wrong way, and tonight reminded me that I don't care for that lady. Hey, Angel, you look like you're about to explode."

"I'm really upset with what happened tonight, and I'm going to talk to Gwen about what she said. I'll wait till tomorrow, though, because after all the drinks I've had tonight, I'm sure I would say something I shouldn't."

"That sounds like a good idea, Angel. Wait until you've cooled down." Cara gave her a little wink across the screen.

About thirty minutes after the Zoom call ended, Cara received a text from Angel: *I'm texting back and forth with Gwen and Sophie. Sophie is saying mean things to me.*

Cara couldn't believe Angel was texting them. *You said you weren't going to contact Gwen tonight...I highly recommend you stop texting them both, Angel.*

Why? Angel wrote. *Sophie's more your friend than mine.*

Angel, you don't want to get in a pissing match with Sophie, because that's a battle you're not going to win.

I can talk to her if I want, Angel wrote.

This is not the time to talk to either of them, Angel. Just stop texting.

By Angel's reply, Cara knew she wasn't going to listen to anything Cara had to say. Cara's phone continued to ping with a barrage of texts informing her of things being said. Understanding that this was not her battle, Cara turned her phone off and went to bed.

In the morning, when she checked her phone, she saw a bunch of texts from Angel, the last one saying, *Sophie talked horribly to me, and I will have nothing to do with her or Gwen anymore. When I talked to them, I looked out for you, Cara, but they spoke badly to me.*

Cara shook her head. She would never have handled the situation the way Angel had. She and Liz had been clear last night that they would no longer have contact with Gwen; therefore, Gwen was a nonissue. But Angel could not leave it like that and had to make it bigger than it needed to be, which had blown up in her face. Cara wrote: *I appreciate that you were looking out for me, Angel. I just wish you would've waited to talk to them like you said you were going to do instead of doing it last night when you had been drinking. Why don't I come over, and we can talk about what happened between you three?*

I'm not in the mood to get into it, Angel replied.

Cara gave Sophie a call. "Hey, Sophie. I just heard you and Angel had a conversation that didn't go well last night. I'm in an awkward position. Angel's my girlfriend; you're my close friend, and now the two of you don't like each other."

"Cara, you have only to look at your girlfriend to see why. Angel threw you under the bus last night."

"What do you mean?"

"She made it a point to tell both Gwen and me exactly what you think about Gwen and that I was hurting you by being friends with Gwen."

"Sophie, please believe me that I have never said your friendship with Gwen hurts me."

"Cara, Angel had the balls to tell me that I need to decide if Gwen is more important than my friendship with you."

"What? That's crazy."

"I knew when Angel said that, she had to be fucking drunk. It was very clear last night that she is extremely jealous of my friendship with you."

"I'd like to come by tonight, Sophie, to make sure you and I are good. Is that okay? I don't want to lose your friendship over something that happened between you and Angel."

"For sure, Cara. Come around seven."

Cara wanted to believe that Angel had gone into the texting match with Sophie last night with good intentions but outright making up stuff should never have happened. Cara was pretty sure that when Sophie started to put Angel in her place, Angel thought the only way to get out of the mess she had made was to throw her under the bus to save herself.

Cara sent Angel a text: *Hey Angel, I'm going to head over to see Sophie tonight. She's my good friend, and I don't want what happened last night between the two of you to affect my friendship with her.*

She was super ignorant to me, Cara, and it's weird that you guys would remain friends. Are you just going to ignore that it even happened and that she said she doesn't want anything to do with me?

This is not a texting conversation, Angel. You and I need to discuss this in person. Let me know when you want to sit down and talk about it.

All I'm asking is if you guys will talk about the conversation, I had with her and Gwen.

I'm not planning on bringing it up. I'm going there to ensure Sophie and I are still good and to have some laughs with her like I always do. When you're ready, I hope you will talk to me about it and let me know what happened.

I did talk to you about it.

What? We haven't talked about it. All you said is that Sophie said some mean things to you and that you're not going to have anything to do with her or Gwen anymore.

Angel replied, *Ugh, I can't do this. I feel so stressed with everything in our relationship. Feel like everything always goes back to these types of issues, and I end up being the one to suck it up and play nice. I am going to finish working and will call you later.*

Cara had just finished putting the spaghetti in the boiling water and was starting to flip the frying meatballs for Cody's supper when her phone rang. Pressing the speaker button, "Hello, this is Cara."

"I think Sophie is more important to you than I am."

"That's crazy, Angel. Sophie's my friend; you're my partner. You'll always be the most important one in my life."

"It doesn't feel that way, because you're still going to spend time with Sophie tonight."

"Angel, if you want to spend time with me tonight to talk about what happened, I'll cancel my plans with Sophie."

"You'll end up seeing her another time, so you should just go see her." Angel hung up.

Stirring the pasta, Cara closed her eyes: *Mom, I'm sure you're shaking your head up there…it's so hard sometimes to figure that girl out! I wasn't the one who had the drunk-ass conversation, causing her big fallout with Sophie, but now she's trying to make me feel like I'm doing something wrong because I want to spend time with my good friend. There's nothing wrong with having friendships outside of a personal relationship. I know Angel's insecurities are causing these issues, but just because she thinks my choice to see Sophie is wrong, it doesn't make it wrong. That Angel can make our relationship so difficult at times when it never has to be.*

Cara's phone pinged with a message from Angel: *I always leave these discussions feeling like I've done something wrong and need to apologize. So, if I hurt you, I am sorry.*

Cara replied, *I'm not sure why you think you've hurt me, Angel. You haven't done anything wrong to me, so you have nothing to be sorry for.*

CHAPTER 45

The Straw that Broke the Camel's Back

Cara had been planning the surprise for weeks. Sitting in her kitchen, the waiting was killing her as she glanced at her phone for the millionth time for the display to read noon, so she could call Angel on her lunch break to let her know what their plans tonight were going to look like. She had been vibrating with excitement all morning and in thirty more seconds the waiting would be over, and she could share her date night surprise.

At 12 sharp, Cara called Angel. "Hello, Angel. You'll never guess what we're doing tonight."

"Tell me, tell me, what are we doing?"

"I got us two tickets to the Garth Brooks concert tonight."

"No way! That's amazing!"

"Since our kids are all at home this evening, I've also booked us a room at the Hilton Garden Inn and Suites."

"OMG, I can't believe it. This is so exciting. Thank you!"

"I'll swing by right at six to pick you up. Will that give you enough time to pack an overnight bag?"

"I'll be ready for sure. Can't wait."

After dropping their bags in the room, Cara and Angel headed straight to the hotel lobby bar to grab a quick drink before heading out to walk the ten blocks over to the concert hall.

The speed of Angel's voice and the quickness in her walk on the way to the stadium let Cara know she was excited. When they got inside the venue, Angel said, "Cara, this is such a fabulous surprise and it's going to be such a great evening. Shall we grab some drinks before heading to our seats?"

"We sure can."

Garth did not disappoint in performing songs throughout the evening that had the crowd singing along with him. When he finished the second encore with "Friends in Low Places," Cara and Angel belted out the words while rocking back and forth with arms over each other's shoulders.

"That was just the best concert, Cara. I loved every minute of it. Since this is our night out, shall we go to a bar before returning to the hotel?"

"Sure, why don't we go for one more than head to the hotel."

"Sounds like a plan."

They decided on 'The Bunker' which was a unique underground bar. The entrance was off a back lane, so if you didn't know about the place, you would never have known it was even there.

They found a couple of seats up at the bar and ordered a round. Cara needed to pee and let Angel know she would be right back. She hadn't been gone more than five minutes when she returned to find Angel doing a shot with an odd-looking drunk man. As Cara approached, she heard Angel telling him to come sit beside her on the last empty stool by the wall because she wanted to buy him a drink.

The plan was to sit and have one drink but now Angel was enamoured by the nonstop crazy stories spewing from the man's mouth. Cara asked the bartender for the bill and paid it. She made a couple of attempts to veer Angel's attention away from Mr. Crazy Man and back to her, but Angel was having nothing of it.

"No, I'm good!" Angel said, turning her back on Cara.

Cara had been nursing her drink when out of the blue, the drunk guy started yelling at the top of his lungs into the packed bar, "Who took my backpack? Where's my backpack?" He made his way through the crowd, pushing people and screaming. "Do you have my backpack? Did you see my backpack?"

"Let's get out of here, Angel. This is starting to feel unsafe."

Instead of getting up to leave with Cara, Angel jumped up and ran into the crowd toward the drunk guy.

Cara followed, trying everything to persuade Angel that her newfound friend was off his rocker and that they needed to leave. Nothing Cara said swayed Angel; it was like she was on a mission, and Cara was invisible. Cara did the only thing she could think of and grabbed Angel's hand. She pulled her out of the crowd, grabbed their jackets, and brought her out of the exit door without saying a word.

Outside, Angel fumed. "You can't make me leave, Cara, or tell me what to do."

Cara tried to logically explain to Angel that the guy was not acting normal, and it didn't feel safe to be around him.

"Fuck you, Cara. You don't know what you're talking about."

What the heck was happening? Why was Angel talking to her this way after they'd had such a fun evening together? All Cara wanted to do was get Angel into a cab and send her home. As she walked to the front of the building off Seventeenth Avenue, she looked back at Angel and said, "It's time to get you home."

"Fuck you. Fuck you, Cara. I'm not going home." Angel was so loud that people across the street were now looking at them.

Cara was embarrassed. "People are staring at us, Angel. Please stop screaming at me."

The words only enraged Angel further. "I don't care who's watching us or hears us. Fuck you, Cara," slamming the palms of her hands into Cara's chest, pushing her backward.

Cara was stunned by Angel's aggression and could barely comprehend what was happening. She saw a cab out of the corner of her eye and waved it down. "We need to go, Angel. Please get in the cab."

"I'm not going home."

"You need to get in the cab, Angel."

"You can't fucking make me do anything."

Cara knew what she needed to say to get Angel in. "Okay, let's go to the hotel."

As easy as that, Angel fell into the cab's back seat.

The ride to the hotel was quiet, but as soon as they entered their room, Angel's temper rose to a level Cara had never experienced.

Getting right up into Cara's face, Angel not caring who could hear her said, "I don't know who you think you are, pulling me out of that bar tonight."

Cara stepped back from her. In a calm voice, she said, "What are you doing, Angel? Why are you acting like this?"

Angel quickly grabbed for a lamp sitting high up on a bureau, standing tiptoe to reach it. Having the base firmly in her hands, she tried everything in her power to rip it from the wall, but the plugged-in chord held it in place.

Cara grabbed the lamp out of Angel's hands and put it back on top of the bureau. "Please stop, Angel. Please just stop."

Angel was completely out of control. Nothing Cara said or did could snap her out of the rage intensifying with every moment that passed. Angel's attention went from the lamp to what was behind the closet door. Sliding it open, she began ripping at the wire-shelving unit, trying to tear it from the wall. When she realized the shelving was firmly attached, and no amount of pulling was going to rip it out, she released her grip and turned toward Cara, going at her full force, slamming her hands against Cara's chest, pushing her up against the wall.

Still, in a lowered voice, Cara said, "Angel, you need to stop. What are you doing?" She was sure that with all the noise, someone nearby would call security. Not wanting to elevate the situation any more than it already was, she kept repeating in a voice as calm as she could muster, "Angel, you need to stop. Please stop what you are doing."

"Fuck you, Cara. I can do whatever I want."

"You need to stop, Angel. People are going to hear you. What are you doing?"

It was as if a switch had shut off inside Angel's head, because she stopped, grabbed her bag, and left the room without saying another word.

All Cara thought at that moment was thank God the madness had stopped. Her body started to shake, and her mind was going a mile a minute trying to make sense of what had just occurred.

Her phone pinged with a message from Angel: *You're not my person.*

Turning her phone off, Cara climbed into the hotel bed with her clothes still on. She faded in and out throughout the night. When she finally sat up due to the brightness of the morning sun, she went to the bathroom mirror and was met with bloodshot eyes reflecting at her. Had this all been a horrible nightmare?

When she picked up her phone, the barrage of texts told her it wasn't.

You are my person.
I don't know what happened last night.
I'm so sorry, Cara.
Please forgive me.
Call me as soon as you're up.

Cara went over and over everything that had happened the night before. *What was wrong with Angel? Why had she acted that way? Why had she once again turned a wonderful outing into a hellish night?*

After almost an hour of getting her thoughts in order, Cara dialled Angel's number.

"OMG, Cara, I'm so sorry for how I acted. I don't know what came over me. I couldn't stop myself. I tried everything to get a reaction out of you, and when you wouldn't give me one, I just kept going and going to try and get one from you. I'm so sorry, Cara. Please forgive me."

Cara took a deep breath. "Angel, I was very clear with you about my boundaries when you asked to come back into my life. I told you then that if you ever disrespected me like you had in the past, you and I would be over for good. I need you to know I'm done trying to make things work between us! I'm done chasing you for your time and attention and I'm done allowing you to treat me the way you have. You physically attacking me last night was the final straw."

"But it only happened once."

"Listen to yourself, Angel. You think what you did was okay because it only happened once. There is something seriously wrong with you. What about all the verbal abuse? All the fuck you, Cara you said to me last night. That was certainly not the first time that happened. Even your youngest daughter has witnessed you verbally abusing me. What about the disrespect to me when men are around, and you ignore me? Last night was not the first time for that, either. You've done that to me even in front of your sister, never once apologizing to me. What about all the mental abuse you have put me through over the years, telling me repeatedly you needed time to figure things out, and me waiting around while you decided my future? From the very beginning of our relationship, you told me no one ever fought for you. Even if you can't see it, I've always fought for you, Angel, trying to do everything you've asked of me in the hope that one day, you would figure your shit out, and realize what an amazing partner I am. It's too bad, that you've always needed to be right over what's right for the relationship. I thought it was you I needed so I wouldn't be alone, but I have never felt more alone than in this relationship with you."

"Well, maybe if you hadn't agreed to go out for drinks after the concert, Cara, none of this would've happened."

"See, this is what you do, Angel. You treat me like shit and then try to make it look like it's my fault. You haven't even heard a word of what I just shared with you."

"That's all in your head. I don't do that!"

"Yes, Angel, yes you do! My mistake has been allowing it. I have allowed you to control and manipulate me throughout our relationship. I have allowed you to choose to be with me only when it's convenient for you. I take full responsibility for allowing what I have, but today that all ends. You don't deserve me, Angel, and I'm done being your doormat." Ending the call, Cara gathered her stuff and headed home.

When she was all settled in, she opened her Facebook page and found a post from Angel: *Was there ever really a friendship or a meaningful relationship if it ends because of one mistake? Things that make you go "hmmm."*

Cara realized at that moment her decision to end the relationship once and for all was the right choice. Angel was never going to change; she would play the victim role right to the end. The writing was on the wall in neon lights this time. The only thing that truly mattered to Angel was Angel.

To make sure Angel knew how serious she was that they were over, Cara took off the ring Angel had given her on her birthday and shoved it into an envelope with a note underlined in capital letters: *I WILL NEVER SETTLE IN LIFE AGAIN*. She addressed it to Angel, stamped it, and immediately deposited it into a mailbox.

CHAPTER 46

Truth

Cara hadn't been in the mood to socialize but with Lila continuing to ask her every other week to come over for lunch, Cara finally gave in and said she would meet her and Sophie today. Pulling up to Lila's house she whispered to herself, "You got this."

Lila met her at the door with open arms and hugged her tightly. "I love you my friend and I'm glad you came today."

"I know it's only been three months, Cara, but seriously, thank fuck she's out of your life. Kicking that psycho bitch out the door, was honestly the best thing you've done for yourself."

"It hasn't been easy, Sophie," looking down and fiddling with a little thread hanging from her top. "When I broke up with Angel, I was still in love with her and that's been a hard pill to swallow."

"Cara, hopefully, one day you will find someone who will love you how you deserve to be loved. The way you love with all your heart."

"I appreciate that, Lila, and thank you both for always being there for me. Heck, I almost lost you because of her, Sophie."

"It would take more than that jealous, manipulative cunt to split you and me up, Cara. You're the peanut butter to my jelly, the ham to my sandwich, the burger to my fries."

Lila rolled her eyes. "Um, okay, Sophie, I think we get it," winking at Cara.

Cara looked at them both. "I need to tell you guys something that I'm pretty sure is going to blow your minds."

Lila and Sophie, in unison, "Tell us!"

"Dani showed me a post on Facebook this morning. You're not going to believe this, but Angel's dating a guy."

"No fucking way!"

"Not only that, Sophie, she's living with him."

"You can't be serious."

"I swear to you, Lila, she had a man move in with her two months after I told her I would never be in a relationship with her again."

"Holy Fuckballs, Cara. That's insane."

"I know, Sophie but it doesn't surprise me in the least. Angel has always been a reactive decision-maker. Since I made it crystal clear that I was no longer an option, she needed someone to fill that hole, and that poor guy is it."

"That is fucking crazy."

"I couldn't agree with you more, Sophie, but it's just one more thing that proves to me that my relationship with Angel was nothing but a fat lie. She manipulated and controlled me like a puppet on strings. You guys have no idea how many times Angel told me how thankful she was that we were together so she would never have to be with a man again. It was a running joke between us that if we ever had to get a guy to do something for us, like fix our car tire or whatever, we'd make this motion with our hand like we'd have to give him a blowjob to get him to help us out… we'd make a fist with one hand holding the pinkie against our left cheek, making our tongue push out against the inside of the other cheek, motioning back and forth the way a blowjob looks just to gross each other out, all because we couldn't think of having to do anything worse and here she is choosing to be with a man again."

"If you ever see her, what will you say?" Lila asked.

"If I ever see her again, I'm not going to say a word. I'm just going to look at her and make that hand motion. She'll know exactly what I'm thinking!"

"OMG, I'd give my left tit to see the look on her face if that happened. I'm going to put it out to the universe, Cara that you get the chance to do that. It would be poetic justice at its finest."

Lila took hold of Cara's hand. I know we're making light of what you just found out, but I'm sorry that you had to hear about this because I'm sure it's all been extremely hurtful."

"It hurt me, Lila. I'd be lying if I said it didn't. Angel always talked about us moving in together one day, and now she's living with a man. I just keep telling myself, 'Thank God that lying narcissistic piece of shit is no longer in my life.'"

"Karma's a bitch, Cara, and she just gave Angel exactly what she deserves…sucking dick and hairy balls."

All three of them laughed out loud at Sophie's comment.

"Guys, no one ever really knows what happens behind closed doors except the two people behind those doors. I'm sure Angel is drowning him in everything she thinks he wants to hear and is giving him whatever he needs just so she can hook him. It's her pattern! It won't be long before the real Angel appears and then the emotional roller-coaster ride for her new guy will begin. She'll tell her family a few negative things about him so she has something to use against him later on, but she'll also tell them how great the relationship is now because she needs everyone to think she's capable of having a good relationship. The truth is, she'll never be in a healthy relationship. Dr. Kendra told me the pattern repeats with each new partner because narcissists live in their clouded reality where they are never the problem, and everything they do is right. She will continue hurting good people because she'll never do the work that is needed."

Lila squeezed Cara's hand. "I'm sure that's exactly what she's doing, Cara."

"That poor guy doesn't have a chance with that lying bitch."

"I know this wasn't taking the high road, guys, but I messaged him today."

Simultaneously, "You did what?"

"Yup. I know I probably shouldn't have but sending him a private message on Facebook not only gave him a heads-up about Angel, but for me, it felt like the final thing I needed to do for my closure."

"I can't believe you had the balls to do that, Cara, but I think it's awesome because it's kind of a 'Fuck you' to Angel for all her lies to you."

"It didn't do any good, Sophie. He didn't believe me and replied with a very aggressive message saying I'm fucking crazy."

"No surprise there, Cara." Lila rubbed Cara's shoulder. "Angel already has him believing her lies."

"And get this: Angel copied my message and sent it to my kids, my niece, and even a couple of my friends, saying she needed to block them now from her social media so I wouldn't see what was going on in her life."

"Seriously, Cara!"

"No word of a lie, Lila. You guys both know that I blocked all her social media after breaking up with her. I never look at her Facebook or Instagram posts because unlike her, if I were to see her with someone it would hurt me."

"I wish she'd never come into your life."

"Thank you, Lila. That's not all she did. She also told them… she was worried for my mental health."

"Holy fuck, Cara, she's one messed-up bitch."

"I know, right? Somewhere in that screwed-up brain of hers, she thinks people in my life will believe her lies. None of what she said or did today matters, because everyone important to me knows the truth…she's just a big joke to all of us."

"Doing what she did only proves what a horrible human being she is. She could have easily ignored your message, Cara, but she knows it's the truth, and to cover her ass for all the shit she's done to you, she needs to lie and tell everyone you're the crazy one," Lila said as she moved her hand from Cara's shoulder to her hand squeezing it.

"I'm sure she's also told her family lies about me to make herself look like the victim."

Lila looked into Cara's eyes. "Anyone who knows you, Cara, including Angel's family, knows what an amazing person you are and if someone as kind and loving as you dumped Angel, people will know who the real problem is. Her family has to support her because they're her family, but trust me, Cara, they're not stupid. They know the truth."

"Thanks for saying that, Lila. That's something that has bothered me. I became very close to some of her family and even some of their friends. I lost them all when I ended the relationship with Angel."

"Right now, Cara, her family is probably thankful as fuck that she's someone else's problem."

"You two are just the best friends ever. I love you guys!"

CHAPTER 47

Blinded No More

Looking through the floor-to-ceiling windows of her condo at the clear blue sunny skies had Cara feeling energized and alive. She'd just returned from her second solo month-long holiday, and today she sat on her couch reflecting and appreciating all the amazing people and things that blessed her life.

Dani was in her second year of university and working part-time at a job she hoped would be her career upon graduating. Cody was working full-time trying to save as much money as he could so he could start investing in real estate. Lila had bought a house in Arizona with her Dad, where they spent their winters together. Having Lila away those months didn't affect their friendship whatsoever as their bond was lifelong; no space or time would ever tear them apart. Sophie…well, Sophie would always be Sophie, wild and fun.

Cara felt her mom with her today. *You know what, Mom? The best gift I ever gave myself was taking these last two years to be alone. Who would have guessed that my greatest fear was exactly what I needed? Having time on my own to process everything opened my eyes. The red flags were there from the beginning, and I learned a very hard lesson, from what I chose to ignore. I had Angel on a pedestal she never deserved to be on. I gave my love to someone incapable of loving me in return, and by finally removing my rose-coloured glasses, I was able to see her true toxic character.*

I'm in control of my life now, Mom. I know my worth, and I will never settle again. Never will I be someone's option, convenience, or second choice. I now know what I deserve and what I bring to the table. If my newfound boundaries are being crossed, it's like Ariana Grande says: Thank you, next!

Mom, I'm so thankful Dr. Kendra encouraged me to write about all my experiences. Writing was so cathartic for me! It opened my eyes not only to the craziness of the relationship I was in but also helped me to forgive myself for what I had allowed. Forgiving myself was a hard one because I stayed in that relationship way longer than I ever should have. I've finally come to terms that I cannot change my past and that my future is going to unfold however it's meant to unfold. I now realize that living in fear as I had been, especially when I had no idea what the future would bring, served no purpose. I now know that living in the moment is where I need to stay and be present. That is what will keep me moving forward.

Cara beamed when she heard the clickety-clack of the mass transit train racing past her condo. Opening the patio door and stepping into the summer's heat, she noticed a dragonfly hopping from flower to flower in one of her cedar plant beds. Cara smiled to herself. "Mom," she said aloud, "I've got this!"

Milton Keynes UK
Ingram Content Group UK Ltd.
UKHW042051281223
434995UK00024B/250/J